Steph

Beast Control
Crossroads V

CROSSROADS SERIES: PART V

Four more short stories from Stephen King's "Crossroads" series that will help keep you entertained late into the night. Discover the bright imagination, suspense, thrilling drama, picturesque visions, and a deeper look into the true landscape of the "Crossroads" series.

Follow the series to piece together the hidden meaning in the stories to determine the overall message that is being portrayed. Will it bring enlightenment? Will it be the light at the end of the tunnel? Does fear take over and leave the message hidden? The journey continues and the message will surely begin to appear and keep you in its grasp.

Copyright © 2014 by Stephen King

Manufactured in the United States of America
Designed by Magic Pen Designs

The Visitor

New arrivals to Saint Christopher's Home for Wayward Girls were told lies from the very beginning. Parts were true, to be fair; it *was* a bit like living in a medieval castle, what with the building's towering stone spires and carefully maintained cobblestone walkway. When they arrived, as they always did, by a yellow-brown school bus that belched black smoke from its exhaust pipe, Abigail could see a glint of hope blossom in their eyes as they looked at their new home. You could almost see when they allowed themselves to believe that perhaps this was what grown-ups would call *a new start*. Somewhere they could feel safe, warm, and take the first steps toward a life that was better than the horrific circumstances that had driven them to an orphanage in misty, mostly abandoned farm country. Abigail almost didn't want to tell them the truth, but she knew it was important they knew about what had been rumored to happen at lights out time. To know gave them the best chance.

Most often, there was nothing strange or terrifying of which to speak. When it was time to sleep, Sister Miranda shuffled into the great long room where all the girls' bunks were lined up, and announced dispassionately that the time had come again to dream sweet, restorative dreams of the Lord their God. She announced this information with a distant tired frown that also informed them all that they had better pipe down right that instant before she grew even less friendly than her norm. It usually did the trick.

"There's nothing more any of you need to say at an hour like this," she announced, her voice echoing off the tall ceilings and the dirty tile floors. The din briefly rose around her as pilfered, dated magazines were stuffed into under-bed cubbies and notebooks with elaborately scripted letters to pen pals - some real and others the saddest possible figments of lonely imaginations - were squirreled under the covers for continued work by flashlight. "And if by chance there is some great insight you must share," Sister Miranda continued. "Please do so as you would any other conversation with our Lord and Savior - silently."

At this point Abigail would hop into her single bed, clutching both her fat yellow flashlights with the overhand grip and the stuffed crocodile with which she'd slept - or sometimes been unable to sleep - for as long as she could remember. She'd pull the stiff covers over her body, insulating herself from the noise of bunk mates whispering and giggling. Abigail took great pains at lights out not to giggle or carry on.

At eleven, she was positioned with the rest of the oldest girls in residence at the orphanage. Their beds were clustered closest to the doorway, adjacent to Sister Miranda's room, and she had no interest in misbehaving directly beneath the nose of the woman who carried the disciplinary ruler. When her rapidly aging ears picked up on something improper, Sister Miranda was quick to bring down sharp retribution in the name of the Lord. This propensity toward physical violence made her a woman to avoid the bad side of, but it also, Abigail reasoned, made her the best possible protection. Certainly better than the crocodile, which, though it made a shamefully childish part of her feel better, would offer nothing compared to an adult that could brandish a small weapon or, better yet, a telephone.

There was a panel of light switches on the dull gray wall, and Sister Miranda lifted her gnarled hands to it. She clicked off the switches one by one, plunging twenty-foot sections of the long hallway into complete, unassailable black. Abigail hid under the covers now, but in earlier days she had watched the rest of the room at this moment, and had thought fearfully that it was like watching darkness itself take monstrous, stuttering steps toward where she lay. Now she didn't watch at all.

Instead, after Sister Miranda let the door click softly closed behind her, Abigail tried to do nothing more than breathe evenly and deeply, taking comfort in the sounds of the girls around her - some friends, some less than friends - spurred back into whispering excitedly by the elderly nun's departure. For some of them, their time here was short enough that they could convince themselves it was an extended sleepover. Abigail had managed to make it two years; she no longer allowed herself that illusion. Even as she felt herself drifting toward sleep, after thirty minutes or so, she felt a distant part of her on permanent alert, ever on guard.

In her last moments before falling asleep, she thought of the new girls again; nine came on the latest bus, herded up the front steps and into the bunks like cattle. She thought of how they were probably awake, too, wondering how this place would work out, and whether it was better or worse than other stops they had made on whatever winding paths had led them to this moment. Abigail hadn't had a chance to take stock of them between the time of their arrival, orientation, and time for lights out. That meant she hadn't been able to find the time to tell them what, precisely, kept a portion of her subconscious scanning her surroundings like a lighthouse on a windy, seemingly deserted shoreline.

She was not listening for Sister Miranda, barging into the room noisily, reprimanding them with theatrical fire and brimstone for refusing to straighten up, fly right, and behave appropriately. No, Abigail did not sleep soundly at Saint Christopher's because she believed that someday, again she would awaken to the sound of the front window, by where the youngest of the girls slept, squeaking open again.

＊＊＊＊＊＊＊

It did not happen, the horror that Abigail remembered and few others believed, that night, and Sammy, as she tended to do, wanted to take all the credit. Sammy was a boisterous, rotund nine year old with an unnatural degree of strength; she was like a bowling ball spinning out of control, in terms of her physical presence and, somehow, her personality. Her thoughts blurted out of her head with no warning or forethought, and while Abigail had come to tolerate her - and perhaps, begrudgingly, even develop a certain reluctant fondness, as one might for a younger sibling it was easy to pick on - Sammy's belief that she was the guardian of all the girls at Saint Christopher's was embarrassing.

"I did it again, Ab," she said, slamming down her lunch tray and then widening her eyes conspiratorially at the volume of the noise it made. She lowered her voice to a stage whisper that everyone else at the circular plastic table Abigail had chosen could hear. "I kept him away."

"I'd stay away from a girl with breath like yours, too," Abigail mused.

Sammy, through a mouthful of mashed potatoes, protested dramatically. "Hey, shut up!"

The other girls laughed. Abigail stuck her tongue out, and Sammy opened her mouth and revealed her disgustingly chewed food. They laughed more.

There were five of them, including Abigail and Sammy, clustered together at most lunches. Tara and Tyra, the twins who finished each other's sentences and were occasionally quite difficult to tell apart, sat to Abigail's left. To her right was Violet, a diminutive redhead that'd been at Saint Christopher's as long as Abigail. That long tenure was the common thread that drew them together - other than Sammy, who glommed on to the group simply because of a seemingly magnetic attraction to Abigail. From the first day Sammy had arrived, she followed Abigail, grinning with the brave enthusiasm of the profoundly dumb. The rest had been there two years or more, and knew what Abigail did. They waited today to catch the eye of any new girls.

"Do you guys see any of them?" Violet said.

Tara and Tyra both muttered *no, uh-uh* at once, shaking their heads and scanning the room. There were around eighty girls who made up the population at Saint Christopher's, and so it was difficult to find anyone amongst the clamoring crowd at lunch time. They'd purposefully kept three chairs open - not that there was anyone else climbing all over themselves to sit with Abigail and company - if they could find a few of the new arrivals. Then, Violet pointed.

"There, coming out of line now. I remember the frizzy one, with the bangs coming off of the bus yesterday," Violet said. Abigail and the rest of the girls looked and spotted her; Sammy started to point and gesture, but Abigail slapped her hand lightly and told her to be calm. "She looks right, maybe."

"Don't scare her away, creep," Abigail said, gently.

"You're the big creep."

"Shush." Abigail straightened in her chair as she watched the new girl approach them; she had deep brown eyes that looked as if they were formed with volcanic stone, and the Saint Christopher's uniform she'd been given looked to be comically ill-fitting, with the skirt trailing across the floor at her feet and her shirt bunching in spots at her impossibly thin midsection. Everything about her looked fragile, and out of place - as if someone were wheeling a glass figurine across the lunch room. "Hey, new girl," Abigail called.

She looked, caught sight of them, and then glanced around the rest of the room, weighing her options. After twenty seconds or so of further indecision, the new girl walked over and sat down next to Sammy, flashing a tight line of a smile. "Hi," she said.

"You're new," Sammy giggled. Violet poked her in the ribs, but this just set Sammy to giggling even more incessantly.

"Don't mind her," Abigail said. "Sammy's with us. Me, Violet, Tyra and Tara. We hang out, have lunch, that kind of stuff. Other stuff, no big deal."

"Okay," the new girl said, uncertain.

"What's your name?"

"Erin Elizabeth Thompkins," she said. She'd had practice stating her name in any number of interviews on her way here with lots of frowning adults, with clipboards and suits, Abigail imagined. She felt for Erin from the beginning; she remembered her own arrival, frightened and alone. "Old nuns could barely find my name on their lists when I got here," Erin said.

"Hey Erin," Violet said. Everyone else at the table offered quiet, somewhat sheepishly polite greetings. None of them were sure how this would go; most times they got laughed at or run away from immediately. That was how they'd ended up being a group of only five.

"Where are you from?" Abigail said.

"Lots of places," Erin said, moving green beans around on her tray. "They were all bad."

Silence descended around the table, cutting each of them off from the other uncomfortably. This was the adjustment that had to be made at the beginning for everyone; confronting the fact that everyone had come from shit, and willingness to up and enthusiastically join a social group was sometimes hard to come by. Another moment passed painfully with Abigail unsure of what to say next to avoid pissing Erin off or driving her away.

"They all had better food than this, though," she said. They burst into the explosive, relieved laughter that arrived like a sudden wave only after the departure of significant tension. Erin looked around the table, and then directly into Abigail's face. Her gaze took Abigail's breath away for a moment; she was both strong and frail to the touch simultaneously. "So what's your guys' deal, anyway?" she asked.

The rest of them looked at each other.

* * * * * * *

It was hard to explain all at once, and so Abigail found herself delaying for the rest of that day. Instead, the six of them - it felt good and *right* to be able to think of a higher number - accompanied each other throughout the activities that comprised a day at Saint Christopher's.

Unless there were other, hidden conversations ongoing throughout the day, there wasn't much in the daily routine about which to get excited. The state had mandated that the curriculum - if one could call it that - the residents would be subjected to would be morality-based, and focused on providing a solid foundation for their entry into long-term, stable homes and, eventually, into society at large. This meant that Saint Christopher's Home for Wayward Girls was essentially one big Catholic school - one long, day-after-day session of Bible study interrupted by meals and brief interludes of outdoor activity. *Outdoor activity*, everyone learned quickly, was code for *recess*, which was in turn code *or don't do anything stupid or dangerous, because Sisters Agatha and Marybeth want to have a smoke and look at their telephones.*

"They don't seem to pay much attention to us," Erin mused. They were sitting in a circle, picking at blades of grass. From where they were on the lawn, they could see across the fields that stretched for miles in all directions out from Saint Christopher's borders, and, beyond them, the deep inscrutable woods into which the dirt road led into. They had spent the hours after lunch crowded into classrooms in metal desks, listening to the nuns prattle on about who begat whom, the word of God, and a world of bloodshed and begging forgiveness that seemed at once ludicrously fictional and uncomfortably close to home. It was the late afternoon, but a curtain of clouds had already been pulled across the sky, rendering their respite from learning about the apostles.

"Get used to it," Violet cracked. "All the rest of these girls think I'm just the coolest," she began, gesturing grandly. "But the nuns? They're too old to think of any of us as more than names on their clipboard. Even me, the prettiest and the smartest." The girls booed theatrically and threw handfuls of grass. Abigail caught Erin laughing - *really* laughing - at this point, and it warmed her. Goosebumps broke out on the flesh of her forearms, and she smiled at the ground.

That night they gathered at Tyra and Tara's bunk; it was near the end of the hall, where Violet and Abigail slept, but a private enough space because the twins had the top and the bottom bunks to themselves. There were benefits, they joked, to being related while they were abandoned. They sat cross-legged on the bottom bunk, ostensibly studying Scripture. In reality Abigail had decided it was time to tell Erin what they all feared.

"What does that mean - *someone comes here*? You're not making any sense and it's freaking me out," Erin said.

They shushed her, and Abigail continued, calmly but gravely. She opened the notebook she kept on her lap, spreading the evidence as she'd collected it out before them. There were the names, the dates of their disappearances, and all the details that they'd been able to muster in hushed conversations over the years. It wasn't much, but having a collection of knowledge felt important. It felt like taking action.

"It's happened three times- "

"That we know about," Violet finished.

"Three times that we know about," Abigail repeated, nodding.

There was a pause then, and the sound of the other girls in the bunk hall - talking about their plans to get married someday, or the oddly long, curling hair sprouting out of the mole below Sister Miranda's lower lip - happily carrying on made their discussion and the self-created bubble around them seem all the more surreal and stifling. Violet cleared her throat. Erin looked around at them, expectedly; she was skeptical but clearly interested. The next part - telling the truth - was where things tended to go wrong.

Violet elbowed Abigail. Sammy, Tyra, and Tara were quietly waiting, though they knew the story well. "Tell her," Violet said.

"The visitor comes in the night," Abigail said. "He crawls through the window."

* * * * * * *

It was seven months into her tenure at Saint Christopher's the first time that the visitor came after lights out.

Abigail was starting to believe this was a place where she could feel comfortable. It was a drag, of course - hearing about God and listening to girls she felt little in common with either titter about the most inconsequential things or shuffle around, steely-eyed, bearing their past traumas on their backs like anchors - but there was enough quiet and distance from the city that it became easier and easier to believe a normal life would be possible for her someday. She liked Violet, and thought when they were older they could get an apartment, and maybe go to college. These were the things she was thinking of on the night when she lay in bed on her back as Sister Miranda clicked off the switches on the panel at the front of the room, one by one. The room dropped into blackness.

There was still the distant hum of the overhead fans, and whispered conversations after Sister Miranda departed the bunk hall. One skylight poured a square of moonlight on the tile floor halfway down the room. Far down, at the other end of the hall, Abigail could just make out the other window, which occasionally one of the nuns would throw open to assist in airing the room out (especially after they had been smoking, which even women of God were known to do from time to time).

Sometimes, Abigail came to learn, one of the nuns would inadvertently forget to latch the window again after closing it. They were old, or they were distracted, or they simply did not consider it a particularly big deal. Abigail couldn't blame them at first; the place was in the middle of nowhere, after all. Who would come here? And who would bother to leave, with virtually nowhere to try and go?

Abigail was on the verge of sleeping when she heard a faint scraping shudder - she realized later this was an impact against the window frame - at the far end of the bunk hall. Nothing happened for a moment, and then, just as she convinced herself that she'd heard a trick of the wind or the bunk hall settling, the window squeaked at it was yanked open.

She snapped her eyes open and instinctively her firsts tightened around the crocodile at her side. She debated sitting up and calling out immediately, but an impulse she could not claim as her own told her not to make a sound. Instead she listened intently. There was a barely perceptible rustling now, like papers being shuffled or a snake gliding through leaves and then - she was almost certain of it, her senses sharpened by adrenaline and the fact that she could not use her eyes - the distinct sensation of a footfall. Perhaps not a footfall, her mind had told her - something *unfolding*.

Her mind also told her this was absurd; she was imagining noises and conjuring images because she was still getting used to being in a new place. Old buildings, like Saint Christopher's, made strange sounds against the brunt of the wind, or as the ancient wooden beams in the walls expanded and contracted when temperatures dropped in the evening. Abigail knew she was being stupid, and yet her heart was thumping inside her chest even in the silence that followed.

The dead air was pierced in the next second by a low hiss, like escaping steam. Abigail could not suppress a gasp of terror then, because the sound oscillated, lowering in pitch just slightly; it was the sound of a next step being formulated, of action being considered, of *intent*. Her imagination was not playing tricks on her. This was real.

Abigail was younger then, just nine, and so her bed was not yet as close to the safety of the room's light panels and the door to Sister Miranda's room as it came to be in subsequent years. As a result, the idea of leaping up and sprinting to safety seemed impossible, and screaming for help seemed a sure way to get noticed by - *was that footsteps?*

"God," she whispered. "Oh, God."

The hair stood up on the back of her neck as she realized whatever had come in through the window - though she was still under the covers and cowering, she was sure there was a presence in the bunk hall now - was moving forward, and the sound of its movement had a horrifyingly *wet* quality to it. She could almost make out a squishing sound that made her imagine someone walking with boots filled with watery mud, or something amphibian or alien - something with scales, that stunk of marshland and stagnant, deep pools never bothered by the light of the sun.

She remembered what happened next most vividly of all. She saw nothing but the underside of her bedspread, but Abigail prayed desperately for whatever it was that had entered the bunk room to leave her alone, to simply go somewhere else. *Anywhere else but near me, please*, she thought. Seemingly as an answer, she heard a sharp yelp then, with horror she realized she was listening to the sound of one of the youngest girls being taken from her bed and silenced in one brutally swift motion.

There was the one sound, that brief wordless cry, and then the first girl - Elena Martinez, a New Mexico import who shivered in the northwest damp and smiled sheepishly each time she stumbled over a word in English - was gone. Abigail had waited that night for someone else to awaken, for Sister Miranda to come storming into the room and wail Elena's name through the open window, but nothing happened and no one else came. Even worse, after a long period of shivering uncontrollably, Abigail's body found an inner reserve of calm and she fell asleep, as if she had struggled through nothing more than a particularly bad dream.

* * * * * * *

There had been two other incidents, just the same as the first. They were not bad dreams. Tyra and Tara had arrived by the time of the second incident, when MacKayla, the seven-year-old from Mississippi had vanished, and Sammy had seen the most recent, just three months ago, when the visitor arrived for Brynn Wilkins, a near-mute blonde with coke-bottle glasses. After that Sammy had appointed herself as the group's muscle - at least during daylight hours. More importantly, the five of them had started planning.

"This is stupid," Erin said, her voice rising with barely constrained fear. "I don't know why you guys are messing around with me, but I don't believe you, and this is dumb, to be doing this."

"We're not messing with you," Tara said.

"Not at all," Tyra overlapped.

Erin was shaking her head, refusing. "They'd notice. If something like that was real, and it's not," she said. "Then the sisters would notice people were going missing. They would call the police."

Even as she spoke of the cops, Abigail could feel the doubt seeping miserably into her voice. It was not a pleasant thing, when they reminded themselves of how little they trusted the elements of the adult world that were supposed to keep them safe. To a girl, they'd all seen what interactions with the police could look like, and they were not pleasant. Sammy had seen police drag her mother away screaming in a headlock. Abigail remembered the titanic physical and mental confrontations between her own drug-addled parents before she'd been removed; arguments that had come to blows for years before finally they were each arrested for assaulting each other. Abigail had since come to believe she had failed her mother first by not intervening to protect her, and then failed her father, too, by not asserting his innocence - though that would have been a lie - when child and family services arrived to remove her from his custody. She would not be that failure again.

"Don't be dumb. Sister Miranda is a hundred, and she's this close to croaking any second," Sammy whispered too loudly.

Abigail shook her head. "They know that girls are gone, but think about it. Girls like us? There's no one that makes more sense to just up and disappear. Runaways, orphans, weirdos," she said. "You remember what you said about how they could barely find your name on the clipboard when you got here? Someone turns up gone in the morning; Sister Miranda makes a report about it."

Abigail unfolded the paper Violet had stolen from Sister Miranda's office; it was a copy of a hand-written report that had been filed to the State of Washington Department of Child and Family Services. It listed Elena Martinez's name, height, weight, and physical description, and the suspected reason for her fleeing the home. In black pen, it read: *Suspected recurrence of past trauma coinciding with emotional disturbance resulting from introduction of new living environment and overriding attachment issues*. She handed it to Erin, and as she read, Sammy piped in: "It says she was crazy."

"She wasn't crazy," Abigail broke in. "She was nice."

"After this, a whole lot of nothing happens," Violet said, angrily. "The truth is that one cares what happens to us, out here in the middle of nowhere."

"This is stupid," Erin was mumbling now, shaking her head incessantly. Abigail doubted she would sleep tonight.

"I - we're sorry," Abigail said. She considered putting her hand on Erin's shoulder but thought better of it. Erin looked up and stared at her again now; the darkness of her eyes like holes one could tumble inside.

"Why are you telling me all this?"

Abigail swallowed hard. She leaned forward. "Because the plan needs six of us."

* * * * * * *

The plan was simple. They knew what the visitor did, after all; it came through the window when someone was careless enough to leave it unlatched. This happened rarely, but even something that occurred only once in a great while had resulted in three girls - that they knew of - going missing. It wasn't a situation they could continue living with, and Abigail was convinced the adults would think them insane if they came clean with what they really believed. There was no way to run; where would they go? The only solution was to invite the visitor back to them, and then, Abigail believed, they could spring the trap.

Two of them would have to wait outside in the night, allowing the visitor to pass by them and start to enter. The other four would wait by the window. As soon as the visitor's head was inside the room, two girls would slam the window down, holding it shut from above, while the other two held the visitor's arms from below, immobilizing it completely.

"They should give us enough time," Abigail said. Erin looked at her incredulously.

"To what?" she said.

Abigail looked around, and then she held up her two pillows, revealing the two jagged shards of glass. They had managed to save discarded wine bottles from the recycling bin at the front of the building over the course of the preceding months; from there it was simply a matter of briefly distracting the two or three nuns on watch at any one time so the bottles could be shattered against the back of Saint Christopher's.

"This is crazy, you guys," Erin said. Abigail could see the blood had drained out of Erin's face, leaving her a ghostly shade of pale. Her illusion of safety, established only a few hours earlier, had crumbled before her. Abigail understood how that felt. She looked at the others, and then reached out for Erin's hand.

"We need your help," she said.

Erin snatched her hand away and got up, out of the bed, surprising Abigail. Fear had turned to fury. She stared at them and pointed.

"You guys are fucking *crazy*," she shouted. "Stay away from me. I mean it, all of you."

She stomped away; other girls in adjoining bunks craned their necks to see what the commotion was about. Abigail heard murmuring from all around and knew, uncomfortably, that the attention was focused on them. After a few minutes, they saw Sister Miranda drift into the doorway of the bunk hall. She scanned the residents' faces half-heartedly, but then sighed and gave up, returning to her room as if the thing she was certain she'd find was now hopelessly lost.

* * * * * * *

Nothing came for any of them that night, or any of the next eight. The mood at meals was mostly sour; they found themselves looking into their food, feeling unsettled and far from hungry. Tyra and Tara rested their cheeks on their fists and looked at each other, mumbling quietly in a language only they seemed to understand. Sammy stared into space and broke small things that no one would notice were gone. Violet, defiantly, refused to be phased. She advocated constantly for the plan to move forward, and she sneered at Erin when she saw her, sitting alone at meals or writing in a notebook during Bible study.

"We don't need her. The plan is fine with six," she said. "I say we go ahead."

"Yeah, the plan is fine," Sammy agreed. She felt unmoored, clearly, in any moment in which the rest of the group was unsettled. Aggressive agreement felt comforting to her. They'd all believed Erin would be the last piece, as soon as they'd seen her, and now things felt distractingly incomplete and dangerous again.

Abigail shook her head. "Give it time. We can wait for her to change her mind," she said.

Erin had taken to sitting by herself in the bunk hall, either in her bed or in one of the wicker chairs by the front window, rarely glancing up from one of the old copies of *National Geographic* lying around the back of the classrooms in Saint Christopher's. They were windows into worlds that did not exist for the residents here; there was a measure of comfort to be taken in them. Abigail had been where Erin was now, and she did not blame her for her behavior. She had been scared, too. She was still frightened.

"Screw her," Violet said. They looked, from Abigail's bed, down the bunk hall at where Erin sat. Sister Miranda sat across from Erin in one of the other chairs, absent-mindedly tapping ash from a cigarette out the front window. Erin appeared unaffected by the cloud of smoke encircling her, making her appear hazy and somewhat indistinct, like an idea of a person glimpsed through waves of heat on a highway. "We'll be fine without her," Violet said again, urgently. "We can do it."

Violet could not have fathomed how wrong she was.

* * * * * * *

She had made no sound when the visitor came for her.

Abigail had been clueless; she woke in the morning to find that the bed sheets and blankets had been stripped off of Violet's bed. A pillow was halfway across the floor, but other than that, there were no signs of a struggle. It was not as if Violet had been dragged out, kicking and screaming and fighting as hard as she possibly could; it was as if the ground had opened up and swallowed her whole, leaving no trace. The nuns now were examining her things for clues - perhaps they would for once think it odd that a runaway had run with *none of her possessions*, Abigail thought bitterly - and scanning the fields, their hands shielding their eyes from the sun. They would find no sign of her. The room buzzed as the news of a long-term resident running away in the night - unless you asked the crazy girls - spread like wildfire.

She tried her best to be a comfort for the twins and to Sammy - who was bawling, even though Violet had poked fun at her - and to make for them a safe, private circle where they could have their own space, but she felt hollowed out, like she'd been walloped in the stomach without warning. Violet had been with her since the very beginning. Violet had survived so many other incidents with the presence that seemed to stalk them. Violet did not seem like a presence in their lives that could just disappear with no sign. And yet still, Abigail could not cry. She had nothing left.

"It got her, Ab. It fucking came and got her and none of us did *anything*," Sammy blubbered, red-faced. She was having trouble breathing. Abigail, not knowing what to do, held Sammy close to her chest for a few minutes until she could feel the pace of her heart slow and her pulse stabilize.

When it did, her thinking slowed, too. She thought of a filthy hand clapping over Violet's mouth, and powerful arms holding her disgustingly close, squeezing the life out of her. She imagined her lifeless body being dragged through the grass, her face on the ground, her hair clumped with mud. When her eyes opened, Abigail looked across the bunk hall and caught Erin staring.

She let go of Sammy and steered her toward the twins. "Stay here," she said.

Abigail crossed the room in her stocking feet soundlessly in an instant, arriving at Erin's bedside near the center of the room. They looked at each other.

"I don't know what to say," Erin said.

Abigail fixed her eyes on the window, which stood open, allowing sunlight and a cool breeze in. "It walked right by you while you slept, you know. What do you think it'll do next time?"

Erin shrugged miserably. She looked on the verge of tears, and Abigail wanted to not care, but Erin's weakness and fear reminded her of her own. She felt compassion eroding her anger by the second.

"Violet's gone," Abigail said. Erin started crying then, fat tears rolling down her cheeks. "We're not getting her back. But I can trust you. I've known it since you first came. If you help us, we can stop it, and what happened to Violet doesn't have happened again, to anyone."

Erin hugged her then, clutching at Abigail's back as if she feared she would fall if she didn't find something to hold onto. She spoke into Abigail's shoulder. "Oh God, this can't be true," she said.

"We'll keep each other safe, okay?" Abigail said.

"Okay," Erin said. "Aren't you scared?"

"Yes."

* * * * * * *

The rest of the day passed slowly, sharpening the anticipation they each felt. They'd decided shortly after the conversation at Erin's bed that no more waiting would do. Tonight was the night they would lure the visitor to come to them again with an open window, and they would be ready. If it did not come tonight, they would be prepared each night until it did.

When the sun had set and the moment had finally arrived to shut out the lights, Abigail hopped into bed, just as she always did. She pulled the covers up over her head, and held the flashlight close to her body. In her other arm she clutched at the faded crocodile, and now, with a few moments to herself, she tried to remember where it had come rom, or why she had grown so attached to such a silly thing in the first place. She turned the flashlight on and illuminated the crocodile's snout with it; she was surprised to notice, for the first time in her life, that the tuffed animal was designed with tiny jagged teeth that jutted down past ts lips like stalactites. It was strange, she thought, how you could look at a thing that was so important and miss a detail like that. She clicked the lashlight off and hugged the crocodile closely, breathing in its smell deeply.

The lights clicked off around them. After she heard the door, Abigail, in her bare feet, threw the covers off quietly and set out. She checked with the twins and then with Sammy, projecting calm as best she could and telling them to be ready, and to be careful.

"Sammy?" she whispered in the dark.

Sammy turned to her.

"Protect the twins."

She continued down to Erin's bed and met her there, and they darted through the bunk hall to the window. Abigail released the latches on the top of the window, and pushed it up. This time it slid open without so much as a sound. She climbed through the opening and hopped to the ground outside, landing on the brick patio in the moist evening chill. There was a moment she feared that Erin would not follow her, but then her tiny frame was leaping to the ground behind her. Abigail shut the window again so it was open only a sliver, and then they joined hands and ran to a hiding spot at the corner of the building. From there, Abigail hoped, they'd be out of sight to the visitor's approach but still able to see its movements. They would find out.

They waited there, pressed up against the brick of the building, their breath seemingly the loudest thing in the world. It was a long time before Abigail said anything. It was impossible to know how long they would be there, or if the visitor would come at all. She tried to push away unhelpful internal suggestions as to why it might not arrive again tonight.

Because it's just had a meal, her mind said.

She forced herself to speak with Erin. The truth was that she wanted to keep Erin and the rest of the group safe, and to see many more years ahead with them, far away from here.

"What was it like for you before this? At the last place you lived?"

Erin was quiet a long time.

"Not good. This young couple, they had always wanted babies but they couldn't have them, so they convinced themselves they wanted one of us. One of the babies with no parents, one of the kids with no home. So they got me, and then they found out after they met me that they didn't like that so much," she said. "Did not go well."

"What happened?"

The breeze rushed through the grass around them, rustling. Erin sniffled, and then coughed quietly into her hand like something had been stuck in her throat. Then, matter of factly: "The guy burned me. Cigarettes. Late at night, so that his wife didn't know. I don't know why I didn't scream for help or call someone, but he told me once that he could kill me any time he wanted."

Abigail felt her stomach clench again.

"I felt him watching me all the time, and then, after a while, I couldn't get to sleep ever. I lost weight, my hair started to get all messed up and thin. And so the doctors took me away, sent me here after I talked about what had been happening. Almost dying once was plenty, and now I'm here, so everything has obviously worked out awesome," she said, chuckling.

Abigail put her hand on Erin's arm. "You survived. That's the important thing."

"Yeah."

They heard rustling in the grass and held their breath. Though it began distant, merely a rumor of sound on the wind, after five minutes the sound of a stealthy approach was unmistakable against the backdrop of a night in the middle of quiet country. It was on the other side of the wall, perhaps two dozen yards from them. Abigail pressed her eyes closed, and reached out for Erin's hand. They squeezed them together.

She forced herself then to as move as carefully as she could to peer around the building corner. There, barely illuminated in silhouette by the moon, was a towering figure in a flowing overcoat and a wide-brimmed hat. The garments were all black and baggy, and they seemed to have no form beneath them, as if there no skeleton underneath to support them. The figure had its gaze trained on the window in front of it, and did not seem to have noticed the two of them. Abigail fingered the sharp edges of the glass in her hand. She could barely breathe, and her heart was pounding.

"It's here," Abigail whispered.

"Fuck," Erin said. "God."

The figure reached out soundlessly, languidly and pulled the window up. It turned its head upward, the floppy brim of its hat tilting backward momentarily, and then, seemingly satisfied, the visitor bent forward as if to blow out the candles on a birthday cake, used one limb to hold the hat on its head, and ducked inside.

The window slammed down and they heard Tara, Tyra, and Sammy screaming; shortly after they heard screams erupt from the rest of the startled, suddenly awakened girls in the orphanage. Finally, an anguished, infuriated reptilian shriek exploded from the window, too, and Abigail knew that at least for the moment, the visitor was caught. *Now they'll all see*, Abigail thought.

"Now!" she shouted, sprinting forward.

She tore around the side of the building, yelling, the glass raised in her hand. Erin came behind, poised to strike. The visitor's head and right upper half were inside the window, but it had braced its leg against the building in a last-ditch effort to rip itself free. It thrashed around, and now as she ran Abigail heard the snarling and spitting from inside. *It's scared*, she thought. *Didn't expect this.*

She hit the side of the visitor's body as hard as she could, bringing the glass in her hands down on its broad, muscular back three times in rapid succession. Abigail found herself unable to stop screaming. She felt Erin next to her, striking too, but she could not tell how much of an effect they were having; the visitor was not falling down, even though she felt blood, or some viscous liquid, spurting down her body.

Then, just as she thought they might pull it off, Abigail heard Sammy moaning from inside.

"I can't," she cried. "I can't keep-"

Too late, Abigail realized they did not have enough to hold it.

The visitor gave a tremendous jolt then, and kicked itself free from the girls' vice grip. It's explosion backward sent the bulk of its body careening into Erin and Abigail, who were sent flying several yards, end over end, before landing in the grass beyond the patio. The world receded at the edges of her vision for a moment. She could hear the girls inside calling to her, trying to see if she were alright. Adults were making noise inside Saint Christopher's, too, which meant that help was on the way. She heard Erin, then, too; she was begging for mercy.

Abigail rolled to her hands and knees, her vision returning, but could not find the piece of glass. A few yards ahead of her, she could see the visitor had gotten to its feet, and it was slowly making its way - slithering upright, somehow - toward Erin. She was crab-walking backward through the wet grass, screaming in fear. The visitor's overcoat had been blown wide open; Erin's eyes had gone wide and white with horror. There was a tentacle, thick and green and pulsing, on Erin's ankle.

The next seconds passed in slow-motion for Abigail. She was up and running before she could process what she was seeing, driven by instinct, by adrenaline, by the unshakable sense that to leave someone behind, to abandon them to some horrible, unspeakable fate was unthinkable. She was lowering her thin shoulder to gain some leverage her tiny body could not hope to produce. She is closed her eyes.

She struck the visitor like a wave, the impact of her body against its lower half knocking it off balance, so that it tumbled over into the grass with another startled shriek. She was dimly aware of how bad it smelled, and of the fact that they could make a break for it. They had a chance.

Then she was there, she had made it, she was reaching for her friend's hand. She would not leave anyone else in her life behind. *Erin, come on, we have to* - she meant to say, but no sound came out.

Abigail looked down.

She looked down her own body, to where the burning sensation was blooming, and she saw the glass shard buried in her abdomen. Her lips move weakly, and tears welled in her eyes. The pain was agony. She looked upward from the glass, following its jagged edges up smooth, pale wrists, dirty pajamas, and the black hair that framed Erin's face, her clenched teeth, her desperate effort.

Those eyes, Abigail thought. *So dark. Like a pool that's been hidden in the shade for too long.*

Abigail tried to say something, again, but she could not. Erin met her gaze.

"It's like you said. We do whatever we can to stay safe," she whispered.

And then she was gone, and Abigail was falling forward onto her hands and knees.

* * * * * * *

She noticed distantly when she was scooped up some time later, like a newborn baby, in strong arms. On her neck there was the night air's chill, along with the whisper of hot breath, the exhalation of air that smells of decay. Her head lolled backward like a broken doll, a discarded child's toy. She glanced backward, the strength draining from her, and just for a moment glimpsed the lights in Saint Christopher's snapping on, as if night for them was ending earlier than expected.

The lights are on and the windows are shut tight. That's good, she thought.

As she was carried through the fields, Abigail could feel herself slipping away, but somehow she was experiencing a sort of acceptance, an inexplicable inner peace that she would have never thought possible in the long-held nightmares she had built up of this very moment. Perhaps she always knew it would come. It was a surprise to her, though, just how comforting it was to hear the visitor's hiss, so close to her ear; it sounded like faint air currents, like a house settling down at night, like a place that she had never seen but could imagine vividly in her dreams. A home far away and still waiting for little girls to arrive, in a world and a future much better than this one.

The Cure

It was 1978 and it was the year that everything changed for Henry Jameson. He opened his eyes that morning and wished he hadn't; he felt weak and helpless and immediately wished he was back in the dream world, where things were more peaceful and there was no pain. However sleep hadn't been coming easily for him and his dreams often left him far sooner than he wanted. Often when he first awoke from a dream he wondered if he was already dead and a sense of relief almost passed over him. Not that he really wanted death to come through his door, but he believed it would provide him with the relief he so desperately wanted. He groaned when he rolled over and paged his hired companion, Alex. Alex had been with him for many years and Henry trusted him more than anyone.

Henry was a retired loan officer, a soft-spoken man who just two years into his retirement was diagnosed with cancer. It was an ugly cancer that stole away his last bit of youthfulness and left him bed ridden most days. He was a short, somewhat robust man. His hair no longer draped the top of his head like it once had, which he could owe most entirely to radiation therapy. His eyes were small, in a way that made it seem like he was squinting at you when he smiled, his round cheeks dominating his face. Despite the cancer, Henry's overall health was good; he often took long walks and maintained a healthy diet. He did what he could to get out of the house when he could but every day was different.

Unlike most men in his profession, Henry was wealthy; he had amassed quite a fortune in his lifetime. He could thank playing the stock market for that, as it had taken very good care of him in his early days. It also allowed him the best care possible now that he had grown so ill. He was able to hire Alex and pay him whatever he wanted to be at his beckon call.

Henry owned a beautiful two-story home, with a porch that wrapped around the entire house. It boasted seven bedrooms, three of which were for his cook, his nurse, and Alex. Not only did Alex have quarters in the house, he had requested an office in the basement to work on personal projects.

What pained Henry the most about the cancer was the loss of his independence. He was never one to have many friends, and always spent time alone. His only daughter Clara, his pride and joy, was all he had left after his wife died suddenly years ago. Now that Clara was married she led a pampered lifestyle.

His biggest joy was his family, especially his grandchildren, with whom he cared to spend his time. That was no longer the case once cancer entered his life. Without realizing it Henry had become a burden to the family that he had treasured so much.

He knew Alex was hired because his family could no longer be bothered with taking care of him. It hadn't always been that way, of course. When Henry was first struck ill, his daughter and her family constantly doted on him, insisting that they would care for Henry in their own home. There was an outpouring of warmth and love all around. They were by his side when he underwent surgery to remove the tumor in his brain that was slowly killing him. They were there the day his doctor refused to remove the entire tumor because he felt it could damage vital brain tissue. The next step was to undergo radiation therapy in the hopes that they could wipe it out completely.

Six months later, regrettably, Henry was told that there were still traces of cancer in his brain. His doctor assured Henry that he had time before it became life threatening and that they would try new things, but at any time the cancer could get worse. Henry's family insisted they would be there every step of the way and he thought he had a really good chance of beating it. He held on to that hope because it was all he had, he wanted to beat cancer to not only save his life but to save his family as well.

Those promises soon faded however and Henry found himself to be a burden on the luxurious lifestyle to which they were accustomed. He interfered with their ability to host cocktail parties and entertain numerous guests. Having a sick old man sitting up in the guest room quickly put a damper on their lifestyle.

Clara no longer had the time to care for him; they couldn't monitor him like he needed. He required care around the clock and dear Clara couldn't cope with it. He was not allowed to leave his bed and he liked to have the company. However, his family grew tired of this. To Henry it seemed once he became needy of them, the family distanced themselves from him. Over time he saw less and less of them. When they realized their life would have to be rearranged for Henry, things started to change. Once his cancer worsened, he needed countless pills and constant care. Although on some days he could sprint around the block, other days rendered him helpless in bed, unable to even walk to the bathroom on his own. There were occasions when his vision would become impaired to the point where he needed help finding his way back home. Clara grew bored with the tedious sponge baths, the visits to the bathroom and the hours spent reading to Henry at night. She felt crazy every time she heard the jingling of the bell from Henry's room.

Henry often thought he heard the muffled whispers outside his door of his family conspiring to get rid of him. He wasn't sure if the voices were just in his head, brought on by the sickness. Was he having delusions about his family? He couldn't really tell. He had learned to hide his pain and discomfort in the hopes that they would no longer see him as a burden. He failed his attempt however; the damage had been done. They wanted him gone and they wanted him gone fast. They decided to hire Alex and some additional help; they then moved him back to his empty home and away from them. Clara refused to even consider keeping him in their home with the option of adding the extra staff.

He had to admit that he felt more comfortable being back in his own home, though he felt the loss when the familiar noise of a family was no longer there. He had gotten used to their presence.

Henry pined away like a lover for his family, hoping one day they would return for him. He was currently in remission, but the fear was always in the back of his mind so he never complained; he didn't want it to get back to Clara. He hoped that she would change her mind if she knew he was well and come and be the daughter she used to be.

Henry's dark thoughts were interrupted when Alex stepped into the room grinning from ear to ear. Henry sometimes found Alex to be a tad odd. He was a friendly and very efficient assistant however, and was the best money could buy.

Alex was a highly intelligent and brilliant young man, well on his way to obtaining his Masters in Biology. He was a small step away from receiving his PhD and planned on working at the local university when he was finished. Research was Alex's passion; it was the area in which he thrived. Becoming a professor was the key to having the freedom to pursue his research as it would allow him mountains of free time. Cancer was his Everest and he vowed everyday to beat it, to climb that mountain and be the champion on top. All his spare time went into his research when Henry didn't need him. He had been hired by Henry's daughter Clara as a companion for Henry, a glorified babysitter, as far as Alex was concerned. He was hired to do menial tasks, and basically keep an eye on Henry as if he were a two-year old. Although there was a nurse on staff, Alex monitored Henry and administered medication on a regular basis. Since Clara and her family didn't visit, Alex was expected to entertain Henry as well, which included walks and reading to him. He didn't mind because the money was good and paid for all his studies. Most importantly, he took the job despite being a glorified babysitter because he felt he could cure Henry of his disease. Not just cure Henry's disease but eradicate it from the planet; he was just that good. Henry had a rare form of brain cancer, a malignant tumor to be exact; a cure for it was still unknown. In most cases it was a death sentence, and although Henry was in remission it was only a matter of time before it would haunt his days once again.

The cure was the answer and his days of slaving away in his office were over because Alex believed he had one.

****

Henry sat up reading *The Pelican Brief* in his four-poster bed. He had probably read this particular book about a dozen times. This was his most favorite room, and it wasn't because he spent most of his waking and sleeping hours there it just made him feel cozy and safe. He found the room to be incredibly vibrant and vintage; everything was so personal to him. He enjoyed the classic look of simple cherry wood. The curtains and carpet were shades of deep green and burgundy. Photographs were everywhere, not art, but framed pictures of family on the dresser, the shelves, and every wall. Despite what his family had done to him he still took comfort in those pictures. A picture of him and his wife Ella sat on his bedside table. Just family that's what his space was all about and maybe that was why it was his favorite room.

Henry looked up when Alex walked in the room. "Mr. Jameson, how are you feeling this afternoon?"

"Fine, fine!" Henry replied. It was no different, the same answer every day.

"Good, that's what I like to hear!"

Alex approached the bed, bending over as he examined Henry's eyes.

"God, do we have to do this right now?" Irritation was evident in his voice.

"Now Henry, you know why I have to do this. If the tumor has spread, there would be swelling in the eye, and that is what I'm checking for. You would think I wouldn't have to keep explaining this to you!"

Henry frowned. "I'm having headaches again."

"Well, as long as there is cancer, you will experience the symptoms," Alex explained. "They always go away in the evening."

"Did Clara call?"

Alex shook his head. "No, no. Not today, maybe tomorrow, though."

"Yes…Maybe." Henry turned from him as tears welled up in his eyes.

"You just rest Henry; I'll have the cook bring you something to eat, along with some Advil. I'll be in my office for the rest of the afternoon and part of the evening with my studies. I'll return for your reading tonight. Buzz the nurse if you need to go to the bathroom." Alex quickly left the room, leaving Henry feeling relieved.

****

After the cook had brought his breakfast of egg whites and turkey bacon, Henry slowly picked at his food, and thought about his family once again.

Will they ever come back? He'd forgive them if they would just return.

Surely they could forgive an old man for his complaining. He hadn't realized he had been such a nuisance. He had just been so sore, so sick. Heavens, he just wanted their help!

That's what you get. You complained and they left you. Well that won't happen again. They'll come back, they have to.

His thoughts caused him to tremble as he broke out into sobs.

****

Alex was sitting at his desk, lost in thought. Looking around the room he grinned. He had done very well for himself; he had every reason to be proud. His office, although it was in the basement, was complete and fully furnished. All the furniture and shelving were mahogany, the best that money could buy. Medical books of all sorts lined the walls. He had everything he needed to conduct research; Mr. Jameson had been generous. The other part of his office was where he had established his own personal laboratory. This addition was a secret; no one else knew it existed. He had been given free rein with designing the room, so the addition was added as an afterthought and since no one ever entered the room he felt safe with his secret. It housed all his medical supplies, most of which he purchased illegally, or stole from the university for experimental purposes. The laboratory was home to many aquariums, and cages set up for the rats.

Looking around that laboratory always gave him a thrill; he was determined to be one of the greats. This was his chance and nothing would prevent him from reaching his success. His testing was coming along brilliantly and right on time. Everything was going exactly as planned. The rats were showing immediate improvements, far sooner than he had expected. There were some casualties but there always was with these sorts of experiments. It wasn't hard to adjust treatment for success. Despite the causalities, most of the rats pulled through with mild side effects. These were the ones that thrilled him so much. He believed the ones that lived more accurately represented the results of treatment than those that had died. Alex had been doing this long enough to know improvement when he saw it. He chuckled to himself at the thought of where he had obtained his test subjects.

Every other weekend, Alex went down to the corner of Charlatan and Main, a dark neighborhood where most of the homeless lived. In a city like Brona there was enough homeless around to keep him busy; they were practically around every corner. On that particular street corner he met a young boy. Alex paid him ten dollars if he could catch five rats a week. The emaciated boy was more than happy to help him and hunted rats regularly for Alex. God, if anyone knew what was going on in his office, they'd shut him down permanently. He grinned mischievously. *No, this was too important.*

He'd conduct a few more tests and then he'd be ready to show the world his genius. Alex frowned; his only problem would be how to administer it to Henry without his getting suspicious. He wouldn't allow Alex to use him as a test monkey, even if it did cure him.

Alex paced across the room and pondered his dilemma.

Suddenly a smile crept across his face.

****

It was another week before Alex set foot in Henry's room carrying in his hand a small syringe. He stole in the room around eleven in the evening. Henry lay there silent, but evidently awake.

Henry, I have your medication." Alex moved closer to the bed slowly, as he didn't want to startle the old man.

"I also have to administer a shot before you go to bed."

"What, is something wrong?"

"Don't worry Henry, you haven't worsened. Your family doctor has prescribed something new for you to try. It'll make you a bit drowsy. But other than that, you should start feeling much better very soon."

"Oh, yes... I see," Henry weakly mumbled.

"Now don't hesitate to tell me if you have any side effects that seem... unusual. I'll need to report to your doctor if there is, as it's very important," Alex added.

Alex proceeded with the shot, smiling to himself. *He didn't even put up a fight! He'll be the first among many to be cured!*

"I'll be monitoring you closely, Henry. Your monthly report is due soon, so sleep tight."

By this time, Henry was sleeping peacefully.

****

Alex slowly walked down the hallway heading back to his office. He was brimming with excitement, his thoughts dancing around inside his head. *What it would mean to cure Henry*, he thought with pride. Not only would this be great for his career, but also he could finally cure his sister Anne, who lay dying of the same condition.

Anne sadly was much further along in her illness than Henry because her cancer had spread throughout her entire body, and Alex was frantic to find a cure before he lost her. He wasn't sure what he would do if he lost her.

Oh Anne. How I hated leaving you.

Opportunities like this did not come by every day and he would not pass it up. He felt responsible for Anne, and that responsibility laid a heavy burden on him. Their mother had died shortly after Anne got sick, with the same cursed disease. It had plagued their entire family and Alex could not bear to lose another person in his life. Their alcoholic father, whom Alex loathed, had run out on them long ago, and was nowhere to be found. *Good riddance.*

Thank God for their housekeeper, who fussed over Anne, like she was her own daughter.

He needed this chance; it could be his last before he lost Anne. He refused to wait until the FDA approved it, as Anne would be gone by then. Henry was the perfect solution and he would be cured all because of Alex. Henry's family didn't care enough to be a presence in his life and therefore wouldn't interfere with his experiment. Not that he was worried. He had been testing the cure for years, long before he came to stay with Henry. Henry would be cured, and live a happy and long life. And most importantly, Anne would live.

****

Henry was ripped from sleep and found himself drenched in a cold sweat. "What a dream!" He shook his head. His dream had left him terrified and unable to remember why, but it left him with a sinking feeling. He shook his head again. *What was wrong with his eyes? Everything around him was blurred. After a few moments his vision finally returned to normal. How odd. That never happened before.*

Just then the cook walked in. "Mr. Jameson, good morning! Just in time for a good breakfast."

Good was a relative term, as they never seemed to bring him anything that tasted any good.

Henry lifted himself up and laid his back against the pillows; a wave of dizziness overcame him. For a minute he thought he would pass out. "Oh!" he moaned.

"Mr. Jameson, are you all right?" Would you like me to get the nurse or Alex, perhaps?"

"No, of course not. I'm fine, really." When the cook looked concerned Henry added, "Nothing's wrong, just got up a little fast, that's all." He chuckled.

The cook stared at him. "All right then."

"Let Alex know I would like to try to walk today."

"Yes sir." She placed a blueberry muffin and a cup of tea in front of him and left.

Henry started to worry. *Why was this happening now? Not when Alex is doing the monthly report, my family can't know about this, he thought to himself.*

****

Just before lunch, Alex came to take Henry for his walk. He moved over to the bed where Henry was dressed and ready to go.

"We'll take it easy today Henry, and just go out to the patio. Rosemary left us some delicious lemonade and some Dickens to read."

"Dickens? Son, are you trying to kill me? How many times do I have to tell you, it's *Grisham* or nothing?"

Alex chuckled and replied, "Well, you can't blame me for trying." Holding his arm out he allowed Henry to lift himself up by grasping his forearm.

The day passed fairly quickly, with Alex reading aloud from *The Pelican Brief* until Henry grew tired and was brought back to bed. Alex stayed with Henry until he nodded off, monitoring him while he was there.

Alex was unaware of the frequent dizzy spells, nausea, and mild blindness that Henry was experiencing. As far as Alex was concerned, Henry had improved dramatically. The cancer was still there of course, but Henry reported feeling wonderful, better than ever.

"What a great report this will be, Henry!" Alex exclaimed.

"Oh yes, well... do you think my family will visit?"

Alex doubted it, but he didn't want to hurt the old man's feelings. "Well Henry, you never know."

Alex was really feeling pretty fantastic at that point. Henry was improving at an amazing rate, he couldn't ask for better results.

****

Henry spent the evening in bed contemplating his situation. What on earth could be causing all these terrible feelings? It must be those shots. Alex had mentioned something about side effects, but he never said they would be like this. *Maybe the cancer had worsened, and he was just not telling me. Would that be ethical?* Surely he would have to let him know that. If he mentioned the side effects, that information would go straight to the doctor. And then to Clara; Clara would find out. The cancer couldn't be worsening; Alex said he was still stable.

"Alex will *never* find out," he hissed. "My family *will* come back."

Henry slowly drifted into a deep and troubled sleep.

****

Two weeks had passed and Alex paced back and forth in his office. He had finally made a decision. With difficulty he tried to restrain himself from jumping up and down with excitement. It was time; it was finally going to be time.

****

The next morning, after checking in on Henry, Alex gave the cook a parcel to mail while she was out running her errands. Alex was in such a good mood, he thought he would check to see if Henry wanted to go for a walk. The day was warm and bright and it would do Henry some good.

Alex found Henry sitting on the edge of his bed with a picture of his wife pressed against his chest. Henry hadn't noticed Alex enter and he had a look of despair written on his face. A wave of pity came over Alex; he felt he understood some of Henry's pain. Being separated from his dying sister was a constant struggle for Alex. He could never imagine abandoning her like Henry's family had abandoned him.

He cleared his throat and Henry looked up. "I thought you might enjoy a walk?" Henry nodded without a word.

Alex went into position and held his forearm out for Henry. When Henry tried to get up his body shook like a leaf. He could feel Alex's eyes on him.

"Henry you're shaking."

"I'm just tired."

"Why are you shaking?"

"I haven't been sleeping, I'm a little weak."

"Henry--"

"I don't want to go for a walk!" Startled Alex helped Henry sit back down on the bed. His face had turned a bright angry red and he was breathing heavily.

"I'm sick of you telling my family I'm sick all the time. They don't come to visit me because of you!"

Taken aback Alex replied, "Henry I know that you're upset, and I'm sorry your family hasn't visited. But I certainly don't tell them any such thing. I tell them the truth about you and you have been doing

exceptionally well these past few weeks. Is that why you're not
sleeping?"

"Oh, what else could it be?" Henry snapped.

Alex stared hard at the old man. "I didn't realize. I could have
brought you some sleeping pills; it won't do you any good to lose sleep.
Rest assured I don't needlessly tell your family you're sick. I give a
monthly report, but Henry you've only been improving. Your family
knows that; they know you are doing well."

"Then why? Why?" Alex took Henry's hand in his and held it
while he sobbed.

****

A couple of months passed and summer turned slowly into fall.
The leaves turned a stunningly vibrant orange and a violent crimson, and
Alex was busier than ever. He was so busy in fact that he had been
unable to return his sister's many phone calls; she had called three times
in the past week alone. She loved to chat with him about everything
from the flowers in her garden to the groceries she bought that week. He
just didn't have the time for it right then, not since he had been writing a
paper on his findings with Henry. It was crucial he completed it and then

he would tend to any of his sisters wishes. But this was all about her after all and he needed to complete it. He wasn't worried though; she knew he was busy and trusted him to a fault. If Anne's condition had worsened, she would have insisted on talking with him.

The tests Alex performed on Henry showed that the cancer was in fact receding, which was quite remarkable. However, he noticed that Henry looked quite pale lately. Alex recalled an unusual conversation he had had with Henry a few days ago that left him concerned.

'Hello Henry, how are you today?' Alex inquired.

Henry managed to cough, 'Good, good.'

'I have your shot ready; just lift up your sleeve, please.'

*How odd, **Alex thought,** he looks terrified. Terrified of what? The needle or me?*

'Is everything okay? You don't look so good, Henry.'

'No I'm fine, just a little tired, that's all. I was wondering though, why has this doctor of Clara's put me on this new medication? What's it for?'

Alex was silent for a moment. 'Well Henry, he believes it'll help low things down until they find something a little more permanent.'

Henry had laughed bitterly, 'You mean like a cure?'

Alex didn't respond and turned to leave, but changing his mind e turned back to Henry, 'You'll be okay, Henry. You will feel better oon.'

Henry attempted a weak smile and replied, 'I trust you, son.'

Before he left the room, Henry stopped him with a question. Taking Alex by surprise, Henry had said, 'These side effects, what would they be like?'

'Side effects? Are you experiencing any?' Alex had been quite alarmed at the idea. 'I need to notify your doctor immediately if you are experiencing any.'

Henry seemed visibly shaken by my words. 'No, nothing that serious, just a little sick to my stomach, that's all. I thought it might just be a side effect from that, I'm just curious.'

Alex remembered being so relieved. With this type of medication it wasn't unusual for Henry to feel slightly nauseated.

'That's okay Henry, that's an expected side effect. You will tell me right away though if there are any other problems, won't you?'

'Yes, yes, of course!' He replied.

Alex finally administered the shot and settled into a chair beside the bed to read to Henry until he fell asleep.

It had been an unusual conversation because Henry had seemed almost afraid of the shot. Then he was asking about those side effects. What could that possibly mean?

Surely Henry would tell him if there was something wrong, wouldn't he? He's not that foolish; it's his life they were talking about there, after all. Who would risk such a thing and why?

Just then, the cook interrupted his thoughts. "Mr. Bridger, your sister is on the phone."

Alex sighed. "Is it important? Is she all right?"

"Yes, she says she's doing well; she just had some concerns she wanted to discuss with you."

Concerns? Alex considered this. "I'm sorry Rosemary, can you tell her that unless it's an emergency, I'll have to call her back later. I really do need to finish up here."

With a nod, Rosemary turned and left the room. Alex noticed that she didn't return to summon him to the phone. *Anne must be fine,* he thought. He knew her concerns tended to be frivolous, and he assumed this to be the case on that particular occasion.

****

A few weeks passed and Henry awoke on that particular morning and found he was feeling worse than ever. *God, this could be serious!* Henry contemplated the severity of his symptoms.

He realized now that he would have to tell Alex the truth about what was happening. He had been a foolish old man; he had hoped the problems would just go away when in fact he could be making it all worse. The side effects he had been experiencing had grown far worse, and he was experiencing a dull throb in his lower back. He was greatly dismayed by this and the thought of what could be happening to him hung heavy in the air. He hated feeling this weak, this helpless. *What will Clara think of him now?*

At that moment, he heard the telephone ring. He tried to buzz the nurse but there was no answer. He didn't get any luck buzzing Alex either. Where was everyone?

"He's probably on the phone… I'll have to go find him, this can't wait," he muttered to himself.

Every bone in his body ached as he tried to lift himself to the side of the bed. He suddenly fell to the floor in a heap, he could barely move. Henry slowly crawled out the bedroom door and into the hallway. It sapped every ounce of his strength trying to get down that hallway. His legs wobbled as he rose to his feet and when he tried to take steps they felt as heavy as lead pipes. He had to pause several times before he made it to the end of the hall that led to the foyer. Once there, he stopped again as a wave of dizziness passed over him. His vision slowly cleared, and straight ahead he saw Alex sitting down with his back to him. *Ah, he is on the phone, he thought.* Swallowing hard, he walked toward Alex as if he had new found strength. Henry could overhear the conversation Alex was having on the phone.

"Yes Anne… how wonderful to hear from you. You got my parcel? Wonderful! Have you been taking the medication?" Alex asked.

"Yes Alex, thank you. I always knew you were brilliant. I received the parcel a few months back. I've been taking the medication three times a day, like you said, but Alex, I have been experiencing some terrible--"

Alex's head snapped around when he heard a cry from behind. Henry was a sight bent over and shaking. He rapidly collapsed and crumpled to the floor.

Alex dropped the phone, and quickly ran to him. Grabbing his wrist he checked Henry's pulse.

"Good Lord! He's dead!"

Alex glanced back in horror at the phone he had left dangling, the knowledge of what he had done brought on a new form of terror "Anne…Anne?"

Beast Control

My legs ached as I ran through the alleyways, one after the other as I looked for a safe place, to hide. Terror was beginning to seize me and I knew if I allowed that feeling to consume me than I might as well already be dead. People were looking for me and I didn't think I was going to make it out alive. I was wounded; they had found me, hurt me, and tried to kill me. They had almost succeeded but I got away. If you could call this getting away but I wasn't doing well that's for sure. It's a terrible feeling being hunted; even worse that I was hurt so badly that I wasn't sure that I was going to make it out there alive. How could I have been so stupid? Now I needed to find a safe place in which to lick my wounds and return to a form that would allow a little more anonymity. I could not be found in this state or I would surely be killed. I would be okay once I shifted, but it wasn't going to be easy. I was terrible at shifting; I had no control over it and it often overtook me into a dark side that scared me to death. I had no way of harnessing the wild side and when I was immersed in it, I changed who I was. I was darker, fiercer and unable to handle the aggression inside me. It made me increasingly uncomfortable because it felt like I was a worse version of myself. The dark side took over so much so that I lost myself. I didn't like that feeling, I was comfortable in my own skin, and I knew who I was and who I wanted to be. When I shifted, it changed my mindset so much that I felt like I was a danger not only to the people around me but to myself. What if I couldn't shift back? What if I became stuck in that world, unable to leave? It terrified me; I didn't want to be a darker form of myself. I just wanted to be me. But that was impossible, so how did I relinquish the dark side while still keeping intact?

A sharp pain coursed through me that helped me focus back on the present. My wound was in my flank and I worried that it was going to slow me down enough for them to catch me. They couldn't catch me; if they did it would be the worst thing that happened to me. It's not because they would kill me; oh no, it would be much worse than that.

I could hear them behind me, their hurried steps a threat to me in my wounded state. There were so many of them and I was slowing down considerably. If I didn't do something soon they would be upon me in no time and then it would all be over. I wasn't sure I was going to make it though, as the alleyways seemed to grow longer and narrower as if I wouldn't be able to fit through them. I knew I was losing a lot of blood and it was affecting my mind, making me woozy and sluggish. I grew dizzy and started to stumble, falling a couple of times before getting back up. Fear coursed through my body as I pictured what it would be like to get captured. Torture and experimentation would be inevitable. I would be used in ways that were unbearable to consider.

Running was no longer an option as the blood loss was making me feel faint. I needed another way, something else. I could no longer run; I would have to go into hiding. I might still be found out, but it was my only option at that point. If I continued to run they would surely catch me and then it was over. My wound was far worse than I had expected. My fur was matted in blood and there was a dull ache overtaking my body. I slowed to a crawl, whimpering as I lay down on the pavement, I wanted to go to sleep more than anything. I had to tell my mind not to or it would all be over for me. I tried to drag myself behind a dumpster in the hopes that I would be unseen to my captors. I dragged my body slowly, fearing that my wound was getting dirty against the pavement. Infection was probably inevitable at that point but there wasn't much to be done about it at that point. Leaning against the brick wall of a city building, my body hidden behind a dumpster, I shifted from my werewolf form into the human shape that would hide me from danger. I fazed back and forth between werewolf form and human form before staying in human form. It hurt to shift and I could never go quickly from one form or another successfully. I needed to learn how to shift successfully because it would mean life or death for me.

It was then that I smelled them approaching, the hairs on the back of my neck tingling. They had arrived and they meant to finish the death sentence they had given me. Who was I kidding? There was a lot more they would do to me before death came and death would certainly come. I was not easy to find in my human state however and I sighed with relief when their group walked past the dumpster without a clue that I was so close to them.

I could hear them talking amongst each other. My senses were unparalleled and no human could match me. I could hear and smell for miles; even in my human state they couldn't find me. I could track them but they did not possess the same type of powers as I did. They were only human after all.

"Where the hell is she?" A gruff voice demanded. Chills went up and down my spine; that voice did it to me every time. He was evil incarnate, the sickest man I had never known.

"I don't know, I could have sworn we had her for sure. She couldn't have gone far, since she's wounded after all."

One man, the leader approached the talker and grabbed him roughly by the lapel. He shook him really hard; it looked like his head might shake right off his head. "If one shot doesn't put her down you bloody idiot than you keep on shooting! Don't let me see you hesitate again. We are going to have to hunt her all over again."

"I thought you wanted to keep her, study her. Not kill her. We were trying to preserve her."

The man shook him harder his face growing a bright angry red. "Of course I want to keep her but what bloody good is she to me now that she's gone? Don't ever let it happen again or you will be the next to go!"

"I'm sorry sir; I didn't think she would make it far with a leg wound. We should have been able to catch up with her."

The man stopped and took a look around, peering suspiciously at every nook and cranny as if something had just occurred to him. Had he realized that maybe I hadn't gone far at all? That I was just a stone throw away literally bleeding to death, completely at his mercy? And there would be no mercy. If I fell into his clutches I would surely never escape. The man was ruthless and he wanted me not only as a personal trophy but he believed he could learn how to shift himself through experimenting with me. He and his men lived on a compound, one that would be difficult to escape if I was captured.

I held my breath and willed myself not to pass out. I had lost a lot o blood but being unconscious would not serve me well if he found me. I may not have had a lot of fight left in me but I would still fight until the end.

"We have people at the hospitals now sir waiting; she will have to turn up at one of them. We'll get her this time."

The leader stopped looking around and turned to face the man that was speaking. "She couldn't have gone far, you idiots. I want to know immediately when she is found. She is mine."

I shuddered at his voice, his words sending an icy chill down my spine. The man terrified me. The men headed back the way they had come and it was only when I could no longer hear their footsteps that I allowed the blackness to envelop me.

****

I came in and out of consciousness and became aware of a man carrying me. I was in his arms and it confused me a great deal. We were walking down a corridor and panic seized me as I worried that I had been captured after all. Who was it? Who took me? Could I escape?

"Relax Cassandra, it's me."

I blinked up at him, my vision fuzzy. I could not clear the confusion from my brain. I did know him; in fact I had loved him once, a long time ago before I ran away from him. I was always running away from him. Marco Reese.

"You're lucky I happened to catch your scent while out on patrol or you could be dead right now, or at the very least captured."

I passed out again, not really sure if I was safer in Marco's arms or in the arms of my captors.

I woke again nestled in a bed fit for a queen. I loved that bed, it was so soft and warm and so big an army could fit in it. There was an ache in my leg and I knew the soreness would keep me from leaving Marco's place any time soon. It was sort of depressing knowing that I couldn't just get up and leave when I wanted. I was literally a trapped animal. He probably just loved that. Marco was a mysterious man but he was also a control freak and very possessive of me. He would really enjoy having me handcuffed in his bed with nowhere to go. It was no wonder; at one time we used to be pretty hot and heavy. There were days where we used to lay in bed for hours making love. He had consumed me in so many ways. His scent was intoxicating and we had a natural chemistry that lit our bodies on fire when we united as one. That was one thing I did miss about Marco the way he felt when we connected and how he owned me with his touch. He was a gorgeous man and his animal instincts craved my body, causing him to perform such acts on me that kept me coming back for more. We had been smoking hot together once upon a time, but that felt like eons ago. There had been a time when our kind, werewolves, was not hunted by man. We were the stuff of legends, feared only through old story books but no one had actually believed we were real. Life was simpler then, and so much safer.

That of course wasn't the case these days. So much had changed and I wasn't sure why our clan allowed it. Now we were hunted by the very men that had almost captured me. They had somehow stumbled upon us shifters and sought out to claim our powers. It was an elite organization and they would stop at nothing to get what they wanted. Of course the rest of the world had no idea that the MAN was determined to keep our power all to himself. It was then that Marco and most of the werewolf clans went into hiding. They thought it was the best possible means of surviving. I disagreed but Marco never was one to listen to anything I had to say. He was the protector and he never believed that going to war was the best idea.

He had a rather large home in the middle of nowhere surrounded by thousands of acres of woods. It was considered a safe haven for everyone; they could live there without the threat of harm coming. The property was equipped with everything we needed to protect ourselves. The stock piles of supplies would allow us to live there for many years without having to go out for long periods of time. It was there that Marco and the rest of our clan hid until we could find a way to claim our freedom once again. The problem was I didn't like hiding; I enjoyed my freedom and I wasn't about to be trapped by a sadistic enemy. I didn't just enjoy my freedom I needed it. I found the walls of what was supposed to be my home suffocating. Marco could never understand why I needed to be free, even if I died because of it. The thing was, I would rather die while living free than to be trapped and live in fear of being found out. So I slipped out in the dead of the night, leaving behind the only man I had ever loved and vowing never to return. It had been a year since I had seen Marco until he found me wounded in an alleyway. I didn't think I would ever see him again and here he was carrying me out if the alley way in his arms. What were the chances...?

His voice startled me out of my own thoughts. I looked up to find him standing in the doorway, handsome and shirtless. There was something about the male part of our clan; they always avoided wearing shirts. Ripped too many during shifting I assumed. Not that I minded;

looking at Marco's carved body was enough to make me warm all over. He was delicious and there was no denying he was the kind of guy you wanted to sleep with if you got the chance.

"How did you sleep? Good I hope. I brought you some tea."

"Apparently like a new born cub. You can fuck the tea; you should have brought me a glass of whiskey. How long have I been out?"

"A day and a half. You lost a lot of blood Miss Cassandra Long. How does your leg feel? It's probably going to be sore for awhile." He walked over to the bed and set the tea down on the night stand beside it. I didn't bother touching it.

"Ya well, all work and no play sometimes."

"I'm glad you can find humor in the situation. Where the hell have you been?"

I smiled then. "I've been everywhere. I even stumbled on a few other clans. Not everyone is in hiding you know."

"Then they're fools; we need to protect ourselves. Who knows how close the humans are now."

"They are close. I saw him; he's in the city looking for me. That's who shot me."

"Sonofabitch!" he roared. I thought the power of his rage might cause him to shift but he was the master of control.

"Why in the hell can't you stay put?"

"I can't live like this. We are meant to be free. Your cage is no different than the cages the humans want to put us in."

"Don't be ridiculous. There are thousands of acres for you to roam in freely, so why is that not good enough until we can amass an army large enough to fight back? So many of us have been killed off already Cassandra, tortured and broken at the hands of that man. And here you were right in his clutches. Are you mad woman?"

"I want to see the world. I'm willing to die for that privilege."

"Well my darling you might just get that wish. You do realize he doesn't just want you for your shifting abilities. He would take your human form every night until you begged for death."

I shuddered. It was then that I realized I was only clothed in a black lace bra and panties. What was even more unusual was that I had not been wearing them when he must have found me. *That sonofabitch.*

My large breasts were heaving in frustration, pushing against the bra. I was what you would call curvaceous. I would have been extremely popular if I had been born in the days of Marilyn Monroe. But with the stick figure society we lived in these days curves were not always ideal. Not that Marco ever minded. I could make him hard in an instant. He liked my full breasts and I had an ass that could make a man weak in the knees.

"What the hell is this? You couldn't dress me?"

He chuckled, "No. I like you just the way you are."

"Oh don't even start sweet talking me, because it isn't going to work. I may be injured but you're not decking me out in lingerie just for your own pleasure."

"I want you to stay put. I want you here with me. Out of danger, far away from that man."

"What so we pick up right where we left off?" I laughed.

"Yes. Starting with me making your body mine again."

Warmth radiated over my body as I fought for control of my emotions. If he thought he was fucking me that easily he had another thing coming.

"I would have thought you had claimed another female by now."

"You think you're easy to replace?"

"No, but I'm sure your bed hasn't been cold every night that I've been gone."

He growled then as he sat down on the bed beside me.

"Don't start Cassandra."

"Oh, dare I even ask who it is? I can recall one bitch that's been in heat for you for awhile."

"Stop it. You left. Don't act like I had any say in the matter. We were in love and that wasn't enough to keep you by my side."

"I can't stay here. As soon as I'm healed I'm getting the hell out of here again."

That made him angry and he had a heat in his eyes that threatened to tear loose. He leaned in and his mouth claimed mine in a manner that dared me to stop him. I became wet instantly as my body knew what was in store. I felt dizzy once again this time; however it wasn't because of the injury but because of Marco's close proximity and the fact that his tongue was making me ache for him.

His mouth left mine briefly and he just stared at me. I could tell he was feeling everything that I was. He wanted me, mind and body and he would do his best effort to claim me once again.

"I'm going to make you feel really good Cassandra if it's the last thing I do." He growled this in my ear and I moaned in response.

He leaned in again and slipped his hand around my neck and pulled me to him. He claimed my mouth once again and he tasted sweet and alluring. His mouth was searing hot to the touch and I moaned when he slipped his tongue in my mouth. His kisses were fevered as if he needed my mouth in order to live. I sucked on his tongue slowly, tasting him before I pulled away. He pulled me in again as he was not finished with tasting me himself. Our kisses grew more passionate as his hand found ɪy breast, kneading it softly. He reached around and unclasped my bra ɪnd stared down at my full breasts now loose from the bra.

"God, you are beautiful."

When I awoke, Marco was still wrapped around me as we lay ɔgether in bed. I was a little disappointed with the fact that I had given in ɔ him so easily. But he had a power over me that was hard to explain, ven harder to come to terms with. It was part of the reason why I ran way from him; he could easily consume me if I let him.

"Are you awake?" He asked.

"Yes."

"You're regretting it already, aren't you?"

Yes, Marco could read me like a book and that point was incredibly ɪnnoying. I loved him there was no doubt about that but I didn't want the ame things he did. I was tired of hiding, I wished often enough for a verewolf uprising, for us to claim our right in the world, instead of ɪllowing the humans to abolish us. We were strong--much stronger than ɪey were, and that was why they feared us, why they wanted our powers, ɪnd wanted to destroy us. So why not band together and either remove them as a threat or fight for the right to a piece of the earth? It all seemed so simple to me and yet Marco would hear nothing of it. He was determined to hide and to hide others even though it went against his own need to be alone. It was a notorious loner and a mind that was so mysteriously trapped that I had never been able to break through the borders of it even though I was the closest person to him.

"I don't regret it Marco, it just complicates things between us, as usual. You want me to stay and I won't. I will be gone as soon as I heal. So why get involved again when it's just going to hurt you all over again?"

"But it won't hurt you?"

I sighed, "Yes of course it will, I will always love you Marco. But I don't believe the things that you do. I will not hide."

"Even if it gets you killed?"

"Even then. I want to live, even if it means it ends in death. I want to be free; we were created for a reason. We have a right to live as well, and I will fight for that privilege as long as I can."

"How can you fight properly if you can't even shift properly?"

"Excuse me?"

"Oh come on Cassandra, your injury. You want to be free but you aren't willing to succumb to being what you are fully. You cannot be a beast and tame as well, it just doesn't work that way."

"Who says I'm tame?"

He chuckled and I turned to him, his bright eyes piercing into me. My heart started beating fast and my palms began to sweat. I tried to focus my thoughts once again before things got out of control between us. "No one would even accuse you of being passive or even tame Cassandra, but you also won't succumb to the beast as fully as you should and that's why you are having problems."

"I'm not having problems."

"Yes you are," he boomed, starling me.

He cleared his throat, "I know you long for control but in order for you to tame your wild side you first have to submit to it Cassandra. You have to let the beast in, to understand it because if you don't you will never be able to tame it or have any control over your shift."

I stayed silent, waiting.

"You have seen me shift hundreds of times Cassandra, you know what's required. It's painful but I just let go. I accept the beast. You are fighting it and that's why sometimes you cannot shift completely or you return to your human form sooner than you need to. You have to succumb it's the only way."

His words terrified me in ways I couldn't express. I knew what I had to do but I had also been fighting it all my life. I didn't like the way it felt, how it changed me into a different person. Well...not a person at all and maybe that was the problem. I worried that I wasn't 'me' anymore and that's all I wanted to be. I wasn't the monster that the humans feared we were, but I was still a beast and when that animal side took over it changed me and I didn't like the feeling of change. The feeling of not being myself and losing control.

The one thing I did like however was the power. Being a shifter allowed you so much power, something humans wanted to claim for a reason.

"It scares me."

"I know it does." He kissed me hard on the mouth. He was starting to draw me in again and I couldn't allow that to happen.

"Let me show you how to harness the power and shift the way you want to. You can master your primal urges and let your inner wolf self take over. "

"I'm not sure you're the best person to take me through this."

"Don't lie; I'm the best person for this job."

I pulled myself up into a sitting position. "I don't think it's a good idea. There are lots of people I can go to for help."

"Yes, that's true. But how many of them really truly know you well. Know you well enough to help you to harness what you truly are."

I looked him in the eyes and wondered how far this was going to go. Could I just allow him to help me without getting drawn back into the spell he has over me? He was right I needed to know how to be a werewolf without being afraid of what it did to me or who it made me become. I had to learn to control myself in a state that was completely natural and wild. It was all part of the freedom I wanted, the thing I longed for the most. So why was it so hard for me to let go? To relinquish the control and truly be wild? I didn't have the answers; I wasn't sure why I behaved the way I did. Something that should be so natural for me just wasn't. But I knew that if I truly wanted to be free than that feeling would only come in the form of a werewolf because they were free. Humans weren't the ones trapped, so I shouldn't be fighting for so much control to stay human. I should be shifting the way I was meant to, that's where I would find my freedom.

But was Marco the one that could truly free me? I wasn't so sure. I wasn't sure of much anymore. I hadn't expected to end up here again, in that house, in his bed. I just wanted to be out there, free, meeting new people and trying to make my mark in this god forsaken world. But if the clans did eventually unite, if we did one day go to war with the humans, then shouldn't I be my strongest self? I wasn't sure I was anywhere near strong at that point. So I should let Marco make me as strong as I could be. But was it a trap? Would I be able to leave him again when it was all over or would he expect something in return for freeing the beast? I was sure he would. He would claim me once again and I would never be free.

"Cassandra, your inner demons are written all over your face. What's going on?"

"I don't want to stay here with you Marco. I'm never going to want to stay here. So if you are doing this as some means of keeping me here, hen please don't bother. I won't stay no matter want. I want a life and I want to live not just survive."

His head snapped back in shock and I could swear his eyes watered up right before my eyes. He took my news like a bullet. He nodded his head slowly and took a deep breath. When he expelled it he said, "I would never expect you to stay Cassandra. You clearly don't want to. But would still like to help you."

I stared at him knowing that I had cut him deeply. There was nothing I could do however, no way to help him. I could only heal him by staying and that would just end up hurting me.

"Let's do this."

We went out into the forest area that surrounded Marco's property. It truly was a beautiful place and I wished there was some part of me that wanted to stay there. It was lush and green and you could lose hours walking around. I used to shift, however awkwardly, and run the length of the forest. But I would not be happy within the glorified cage that Marco had made for himself. Not now, not ever. It was an incredible place to live but they were all just hiding, just waiting for someone to find them and I was done waiting. I would be free in the world even if it killed me. I loved Marco and this place but I wanted the freedom to come and go as I pleased. Not be made captive just in case we were to run into the MAN again.

Marco stood there in a clearing in the forest. He was handsome standing in the light that filtered through the trees. He looked fantastic. We were going to try to control my shifting. If that was possible but the whole idea of it terrified me. I hated losing myself through a shift.

"Are you ready Cassandra?"

I nodded. "I think so."

Marco had his arms to his sides and his hands were in fists. He would go from man to beast sooner that you would expect. It's a fast process. "There's no anger here beautiful, just think like a beast and it happens. Let the change happen without any drawbacks. It's your fear that causing your shifting to be ragged."

I had to get really angry or terrified in order to change, I could not just become the beast. It just happened to me, not through any will of my own. Marco shifted with the calmest of minds, and I could not do it without anger.

When Marco shifted it was fast. One minute he was in a human form and then the next he was something else entirely. It wasn't like in the old horror movies with the silver bullets. It wasn't slow and agonizing. You didn't see a person turn into a dog. Your face didn't change slowly, you didn't grow a snout. Hair didn't just sprout out of every crevice. It was just the transfer of one form to another. One minute he was wearing clothes and the next those clothes were shredded on the ground. And there stood a massive beast in front of me. I was so jealous of his ability to shift and to do it so easily. It was something that I worried that I would never be able to master. It could be very dangerous for me if I didn't get it mastered. I could easily be killed mid-shift if I was unable to get it right.

I inhaled deeply. "So, how did you do it?"

"I freed my mind Cassandra, something you should be really good at. You seem to be fully capable of forgetting about me and running off for a year so this should be a cake walk for you. I opened my mind to a freedom that is just like the wolf and I shift. A wolf has a clear mind because it works off of instinct not emotions. You are too emotional, you let fear hold you back, and that is why you can't shift properly. You don't like losing yourself to the beast but I'm afraid that it's the only way. You think you are free but I think your mind is in the cage you're afraid of. Now try it."

It made sense what he was saying, but I also knew it wasn't as easy as that. I tried to picture it, to picture freedom as air blowing in the wind. I let myself picture what it would be like to not have a body at all, to be not a human or a whole being but just like air. Freeing the mind was difficult for me. I fought it so much in my life in general that it was hard to do it on the spur of the moment like that. The air that blew through the forest and left without anything standing in its way. I didn't hear any sounds at all, not Marco speaking or the birds in the trees, the sounds of nature had up and disappeared. My mind was freeing and I felt nervous butterflies moving excitedly in my stomach. It was then that I started to shift. The pain came first but it wasn't the physical pain you would expect. My body was not contorting or ripping in any way, the shift happened too quickly for one to notice a physical sensation. It was a mental pain, almost as if one soul was leaving the body and was replaced by another. That was the thing I feared most of all was losing myself and never getting it back. It made my shifting process that much more terrifying for me because I usually did it in a state of fear or rage. But this time it came so easily that I didn't feel anything but the mental anguish of losing myself.

I was almost there, I never shifted as quickly as Marco, but it was happening all on its own that time. The more I was able to practice freeing my mind the quicker I would be able to shift. I was in awe of the transformation that I was experiencing that time.

And then I heard a sound, one that didn't belong there. One that I wouldn't have expected especially not there. This was after all our safe haven, a place that should never be breached. A twig snapped in the distance. We weren't alone. *Oh god, we're not alone.* Just as I finished my transformation an arrow pierced through my side dropping me down onto my forepaws.

I heard a howl come from Marco but it was too late. I was already hit and he could do nothing to stop it. A growl tore out of me as I nipped at the arrow imbedded in my skin. I needed to get it out of my body in case I shifted back to my human form accidentally. Having it in there during a shift could cause some serious damage. I couldn't quite reach it with my jaws and I was starting to lose a lot of blood. The voices were coming closer; they would be there in minutes. I only had minutes.

Marco appeared above me and he was in his human form.

"Stay still. I have to get this out of you so that you can shift back We need to get out of here."

His eyes darted around the forest looking for the attackers.

"I don't know how they got here. How they found us. We have been hidden for so long."

I wasn't sure if he was talking to himself or if he just expected me to listen to his rant. All I could offer him was a soft whimper.

"Hang on, this is going to hurt."

He grasped the arrow in his fist and yanked it out in one quick movement. I growled softly to prevent from howling. We were already in trouble. I didn't need to bring the MAN right to me. Now that the arrow was out of my body I could safely shift back to my human form. I was thankful that Marco had brought extra clothes for our training session because the two of us were buck naked after our shift. He grabbed the clothes and we made a quick exit through the trees, there had been no time. The humans would be upon us at any moment.

I smelt him, he was further off than the others, probably staying back for safety sake but he was there. How had he found us? There was nothing there that linked the property to werewolves. I had to pray that I had not led them there. But how could I have? Marco had carried me out of the alley way long after my captors had left. So how did they find me? It was all too horrifying. We had an entire clan living there, and they could all be wiped out or captured. We needed to get back to the house

nd warn everyone. Had we been at the house when the humans arrived
e could have been in a better position to protect ourselves. We could
ave killed them from a distance, we had lots of weapons, but there they
ere in the forest, naked and vulnerable.

Marco handed me some clothes, "Here get these on, we are going to
ave to make a run for it."

"Through the clearing? Are you insane? We will never make it."

I pulled the t-shirt over my head and slipped into my jeans. I pulled
ne zipper up and buttoned them. I was bare foot but that would have to
o until we got back to the house. I watched as Marco dressed his
orgeous body in front of me.

"We don't have a choice Cassandra; we have to make a run for it."

"I'm hurt Marco, I have shooting pain all through my side. I'm
leeding. I don't know how fast I can run. I know you're right we can't
xactly walk through the clearing especially if we are being watched and
ve also need to get out of the forest before we are killed but I am only
oing to slow you down. It's too risky. You should go without me. Get
ack to the house, warn everyone, save whomever you can and I will be
ight behind you."

"Are you crazy? I'm not leaving you here alone. They are right behind us, what if you get captured again? I can't lose you again."

"I'm not going to be able to run fast."

"We will do the best that we can do. I'm not leaving you."

I looked into his eyes and knew it was pointless to argue with him. It only wasted time and he would not relent on this. He was in love and would not leave me for anything.

Just then an explosion erupted shaking the ground. We looked towards the house and seen it was on fire. Another eruption of flames tore out of the forest and hit the house.

"Holy shit, they have grenade launchers."

Marco stood there stunned. I shook his shoulders. "Marco, snap out of it we have to get over there and make sure no one is hurt."

He nodded though I saw tears in his eyes. Our clan was our family and they were in trouble. He had always believed that we were safe there and instead there we were right on our own property fighting a war that he vowed he would never fight.

Some sections of the house were in flames and I hoped no one had been killed in the explosions. It would have taken them off guard; they never would have seen it coming.

"Cassandra, what if I was wrong this whole time. What if everyone dies anyways and it's been all for nothing?"

"It wasn't all for nothing Marco, you have kept the clan safe this whole time when many others were wiped out. But we aren't going to worry about it right now. We need to go or we may be too late."

The voices were closing in though they were harder to hear now that there were explosions and a burning house going on around us. Marco made a quick scan of the woods around us.

"Ready?"

I gulped, "Sure, let's do this."

He grabbed my hand and we made a break into the clearing. I heard shouting behind us so I was sure that we had been spotted running away. The pain in my side screamed as we ran. I knew I was not going to be able to keep the pace for very long as the pain began to spread. I was already starting to bend to the side to ease the pain.

"Are you okay Cassandra?"

"No, but keep going. I will survive."

We ran, our feet pumping across the clearing. We were about halfway and I could see some of our clan in the distance leaving the house. Hopefully they were getting everyone out. I didn't want to look behind me but I knew I had to. I had to see if we were being pursued by the MAN. Were they already in the clearing, were they gaining on us? I looked over my shoulder as I ran and saw that there was a large team in the clearing. They were running after us. They were a good distance from us but that wouldn't last long.

"Shit. They're coming."

The pain was getting worse and I cried out as I stumbled to the ground. I heard Marco curse. I tried to get up but the pain caused me to buckle over. The side of my t-shirt was soaked in blood. Marco came to me and helped me stand up. We both looked behind us at the team that was closing in. If they got close enough to shoot us we would be done for. Marco lifted me up and tossed me over his shoulder. It didn't make me feel any better but we were out of options. I had a searing pain in my side and as I bounced against his shoulder I thought I might actually pass out. Too much was happening too fast, I couldn't keep up.

The clan saw us coming and a few men came running to help Marco with me.

"Hey have you got everyone out of the house?" Marco asked.

"Yes Marco we got everybody. They were able to go out through the back and through the woods, they will be okay."

"Why didn't you go with them?"

"We came back to help you fight. We were able to get some of the weapons, just not all of them."

"Great. Where are they?"

Joshua, another wolf asked, "Is Cassandra okay?" He was looking at my t-shirt that was soaked in blood.

Marco looked me over, "She's not good. But there's nothing we can do for her now. We need to get out of here. We won't fight this war now. We will use the weapons to hold of the organization, but the goal here is to get out of here. We can't win this right now, they had the element of surprise and there are too many of them."

I leaned on Joshua feeling a little woozy. He put his arm around me and held me close. I would be useless for any type of a war, I had lost too much blood and I would need to lie down soon before I passed out.

"You need to get Cassandra out of here."

"I'm not leaving. It's me they want. They will keep killing everyone here, until they have me. I'm not having anyone die for me. I'm staying, so let's just do this and get it over with."

Marco stared at me hard but I refused to relent. I was not leaving without him. I did not want to find out later that he died because of me. I wasn't entirely sure how the organization had found us but I was sure that it had something to do with me. Marco wasn't going to die for me. Maybe I had led them there I couldn't be sure. But it would end with me right by his side.

Shots were fired and we all turned around to see my captors closing in on us. It was time to go. Joshua had out the remaining guns that were taken out of the house. We took cover around the landscaping in front of the house. The area was hot from the flames leaping out of the house. It wouldn't be long at all before the whole thing would be gone. If we survived this we would have to start over somewhere else, we would never be able to come back there. It brought tears to my eyes at what

Marco had lost in one night. If I could I would make it up to him, but becoming his sex slave would have to wait until I healed from all my injuries.

I had been given a gun but the best I could do was lean up against a tree trunk and try to avoid getting shot. I was bleeding out and it had made me considerably weaker. I couldn't even hold onto the gun tightly enough. I would only use it if I had to. Marco, Joshua and the others were taking some of the guys down however. I watched as they went into action aiming at the team that was coming towards us. They managed to drop some of the numbers of the men hunting me. I was so relieved that everyone got out of the house alive. I already felt guilty enough without dealing with the guilt of someone who died because of me. The organization started to scatter all over the place to avoid the firepower that was coming their way. It would certainly make it harder to kill them.

"We need to move now. Let's slowly back towards the house and go around the side. We will depart through the trees in the back like the others did."

Our clan made hast and backed away from the area. Some of them split up and went around one side of the house while the three of us went around the other. I had to be carried by both Marco and Joshua. I was dead weight to these guys; their escape was far more difficult with me.

"Marco, can't you guys hide me and leave me behind. Come back for me later?"

Marco looked at me like I was from another planet.

"You will be dead or captured."

"I may already be dead if you can't get me to help quickly."

"She's lost a lot of blood, she's just talking crazy." Joshua added.

"Tell me about it. Cassandra, I'm not leaving you behind. I would rather die myself."

"Well you might get that wish you fool. The house is good, we are low on ammo and completely surrounded."

"She's absolutely right you know. You don't really stand a chance."

I spun around in horror as the MAN walked out of the woods with a machine gun in his hands. It was at the ready so I knew it was pointless to fire myself. Marco raised his however and I cried out. "Marco, no!"

"I would listen to your little mutt if I was you. I can shoot you all in seconds so how about you don't do anything stupid. Drop your guns."

It had finally come to this. We would all either be slaughtered or captured or both. The MAN held no mercy for our kind and he would get whatever he wanted. I was what he wanted so I was scared that he would just kill all the others. I couldn't bear to see them killed, all because of me.

"Leave them alone. I'm the one you want. Let them go."

"Cassandra, what the hell are you doing?" Marco yelled.

"It is true, *Marco,* it is Cassandra that I want. I could care less what happens to you. The sooner your race is annihilated the better of mankind will be."

How did he know Marco's name? How long had we been hunted? He must know so much about us if he has our names and knew where Marco's property was. But how?

"How did you find us?" Joshua asked.

"Ahh, that is the question of the day isn't it," he chuckled. "You disgusting animals have been hiding out here for years. I finally found you, and it was really easy actually. I just had to wait for one of your own to betray you."

"What?" I said.

Just then a tall man walked out of the forest. Julien. Julien had been gone from our clan for a few months now. We had thought he had been killed. He just up and disappeared, never to be heard from again. He just stood there right beside the MAN looking smug.

"I can tell by your shocked expressions that you are surprised to see Julien. Apparently he got sick of being on the losing side. He wanted more from me than your clan could offer. He has been giving me information about your whereabouts and the whereabouts of other clans for months. I would have come sooner but I had my hands on Cassandra for awhile and got distracted."

Marco looked over at me in horror.

"But of course she had to escape and when we lost her I knew where she had ended up. It was so easy after that. Julien has been a great help to us."

"Julien, you piece of shit," Marco growled.

"Oh give me a break Marco, you have been hiding out here for years and we are no further ahead in the war then when we were free. The organization treats me like a king."

The MAN looked at Julien and then back at us. "Yes, that was as long as you were useful to me and well to be truthful you no longer are." He pointed his gun at Julien and mowed him down with bullets before turning his gun quickly back on us.

Tears rolled down my cheeks as I looked down at the body of our fallen clan member. He had made a bad choice but he didn't deserve to die.

"You son of a bitch! I'm going to kill you myself!" I said.

"Brave words for a girl being held at gunpoint."

"Fuck you."

"Come here Cassandra, it's time for us to go."

"Like hell she is. She's not going anywhere with you." Marco said.

"Oh but she is. She has the choice of coming with me peacefully or watching you all die. And by the looks of that shirt she also doesn't have long to live."

Marco looked at me and I saw fear in his eyes. He was so scared to lose me. It wasn't death he feared most in the world, no he feared losing me. Without me he would die anyways.

"It's okay," I said to him, "It's for the best. I couldn't stand to see you all killed because of me."

"It wasn't because of you Cassandra, we were all betrayed."

"Yes but he's here for me and no one else."

"You won't make it out alive either Cassandra. When he's done with you he will throw you away. We are all disposable to him."

"I have to go Marco, I'm sorry."

I started walking towards the MAN when Marco grabbed my hand. "Don't do this."

I smiled sadly, "There isn't another way. I'm sorry."

"She's a smart girl Marco. You don't need to worry, I intend on taking very good care of Cassandra."

Marco growled. Would it benefit him to shift right then? He should have a long time ago. They all would have made it out had they shifted. But he couldn't shift with me injured. I would die in a shift with so much blood lost. And I couldn't get out of there without their help. There was a good chance I would never see Marco again but I needed to save his life because of the many times he had saved mine.

"Cassandra, if you go. You will die; we will never see you again. I will die anyways without you. Don't you see that? I need you. Please let's fight. Let's fight the way you always said you wanted to. Don't give up now. Help is coming."

The MAN laughed loudly, "Help is coming. Possibly but you will all be dead by then. You morons. You have no clue what you are up against and you think you hold any kind of threat to me?"

I shook my arm loose from Marco's grasp and walked towards the MAN. He grabbed me the moment I got close enough and he held me against him. I looked at Marco and mouthed I'm sorry. My back was against the MAN's chest and he had the gun now pointed at me. Marco wouldn't dare shoot now. It was over. I would be captured once again and this time there would be no escape. The MAN never made the same mistake twice.

"It's time we got out of here Cassandra."

As we started backing away from my clan members the MAN swung his gun away from me and fired a round of shots at Joshua who dropped to the ground immediately, dead.

"Noooo!" I screamed. I struggled then pushing back into the MAN until he lost his balance and we both went down. I hit my side hard and dizziness swirled all around me. I heard a howl and knew that Marco had shifted. I hoped he was running as far away from there as he could.

But he didn't instead I saw him above me as the MAN struggled to get out from under me. Marco bared his teeth at him and the MAN no longer had his gun. All I heard before I passed out into oblivion was ripping of flesh and the terrifying screams of the MAN.

I awoke once again within the folds of the softest quilt and sighed heavily. I felt like I had been sleeping for years and for all I knew I had been. It was like Snow White who slept until her Prince Charming kissed her worries away.

I turned my head and didn't recognize the room I was in at all. I did however recognize the man sleeping in a chaise lounge

"Marco?"

He awoke immediately and drowsily came over to the bed.

"How do you feel?"

"Tired. How long have I been out?"

"For three days. You scared us. You lost so much blood we thought we had lost you."

"Where are we?"

"Paris."

I laughed, thought it hurt to laugh. "Paris? Really?"

"Ya haven't you ever heard of the werewolves of Paris?"

"No, not at all."

"Well you have now. We have acquired property here. The house is gorgeous and you will love it. We are going to start over here."

"What happened to...him?"

"Well he's gone. I killed him. I rather enjoyed it too. But I don't imagine that ends things. Someone else will take on the reigns of the organization and we will have to start all over again. Hopefully we are safe this time."

"I'm sorry Marco."

"Shhh...just stay with me this time. I don't want you to be a prisoner, we'll figure it out. But I love you Cassandra and you belong to me."

He bent down and kissed me on the lips. I hoped he was right.

Deadly Ride

There were a dozen men and women behind the tall oaken doors that led to the board room, and in a few minutes each of them would want Carson Phillips dead. As he waited for Tim to finish the initial briefing, however, a recently downsized employee with a nine millimeter pistol was far from his foremost concern; it was the 45-pound girl on the other end of his video call.

"You said you were coming home after you went to work," Claire mumbled. Her face was downcast, and the thick brown hair she inherited from Carson hung in her eyes. She would not look at the screen, and somehow this behavior – stewing sullenly, not shouting or tantrum-throwing – made him feel worse than anything else would have. "You promised," Claire said.

He sighed, scanning her tiny, round, rosy face. Kelly was working a few feet behind her, obliviously banging kitchen pots around. She was doubtlessly planning an elaborate dinner. He could sense the guilt galloping toward him; Kelly would make him feel terrible for not appreciating the plans she had made, and his daughter would shame him for abandoning her to fly to San Francisco to finalize the merger. Personally and professional, he was the asshole.

"I know, sweetheart, and when I get back, I'm going to make it up to you a thousand times," he said. She didn't respond. This was Carson's cue to bring out the big guns. "We can go to Six Flags next week," he offered, his tone rising hopefully.

She peered at him suspiciously through her curtain of hair. "Do you promise? If you promise about Six Flags roller coasters you can't take back that promise," she said, solemnly. There was nothing more sacred to Carson's daughter than rides that flipped her upside down at impossibly dangerous speeds.

He held his hand up in the air. "Scout's honor, pinky swear."

Claire poked the screen with her pinky finger. "Pinkies."

He put his pinky up. "Pinkies," he said.

Claire turned in her seat and shouted triumphantly. "Mom, we're going to Six Flags!"

Kelly walked around the kitchen counter, and ruffled Claire's hair, kneeling at her side. "That's great, baby. Why don't you go in the bathroom and wash up."

"Okay," Claire said. "Bye, Daddy."

"Goodbye, sweetheart. I'll see you very soon," he said. The smile disappeared from Kelly's face when their daughter had left the room.

"Six Flags? That seems – wait," she said. She sighed. "You're not coming home yet."

"There were last minute changes, honey. I have to fly back to hammer some things out with corporate on compensation," he said.

He waited for an explosion of tears or angry words delivered through clenched teeth. But Kelly smoothed her hair behind her ears and exhaled, so that for a moment she looked like the girl he'd met decades ago.

"I'm disappointed, but I understand. You're the president of the company, and you need to be there to see this through." She smiled supportively, and for a moment he shocked himself with a strong urge to reach through the screen and embrace her. He hadn't felt such an impulse in a long time.

"Thank you, Kel. Thank you so much for understanding."

"Of course," she said. As he opened his mouth to respond, there was a loud buzz from Carson's pocket. His hand flew to his side, off-camera. Kelly cocked her head. "What was that?"

Carson summoned a quizzical smile. "I didn't hear anything." The oaken doors opened and Tim walked out.

"Everyone's arrived," he said.

Carson nodded. "I'll be right in. I have to go, honey," he said.

"Okay, I-"

He ended the call. He checked to see if Tim was paying attention and then he turned his back to the conference room and took out the prepaid phone. He hit the first button on the speed-dial.

"I'm about to do it," he told the other end. "I'll be on my way as soon as I can. Okay."

He clapped the phone shut and dropped it in his pocket, and then walked briskly into the board room.

* * * * * * *

"I want to thank you all for being here today," Carson said. He wa seated at the head of the long table, addressing the senior leadership of Brenner Labs. "It's an exciting time for the joint venture, of course, and it was important to all the partners and MacArthur-Brown that we work with you personally to communicate the next steps for everyone."

There were twelve pasty-faced vice presidents at the table with hin and Tim. He could see the uncontrollable nervousness in their sallow countenances. Carson knew that any time a small company with a desirable innovation, like Brenner Labs, was acquired by a larger one with resources and an interest in profit, there was bound to be a certain prevailing concern among the smaller company's employees. Who coulc say what a corporate conglomerate's intentions were, or whether there would be changes afoot? That's why Carson was here – to rip the band-aid off quickly, so that the pain would be over as quickly as possible.

"There's nothing we respect and value more than the commitment you've made to innovative research in fighting the battle against cancer," Carson said. "That's why we've made a strategic decision in the best interests of ensuring your innovation is taken to market as quickly and effectively as possible."

It was always interesting to see if this was the point that they all understood what was about to happen. *Not today,* Carson thought. They ooked at him, expectedly, waiting for the leadership he had promised. Little did they know.

"To safeguard our ability to go to market, we'll be undergoing ome organizational streamlining in the interests of cost control," Carson aid. He was picking up the pace now; his mind was already on the walk ut of the room and the car that would await him at the curb. He opened is briefcase as people began to exchange looks and murmur amongst ach other. "If you'll pass these around, please. What you'll see in front f you is that the ownership at MacArthur-Brown has very generously rovided three months' severance to ease the transition into your next-"

"You're fucking *firing* us?" a ruddy-faced, pudgy woman nearly ursting out of a pantsuit exclaimed.

"I knew it," a bald black man with a graying goatee mumbled, haking his head and clenching and unclenching his fists. Carson cleared is throat and looked at Tim, but Tim was shaking his head, too; he adn't been informed ahead of time, and so the restructuring – even Carson had gotten used to saying meaningless, neutered phrases like this - was angering him, too.

"Heather," Carson began.

"It's Pam, actually."

Carson cleared his throat again. "Pam, I believe you'll find that the package we're providing is far more generous than is required in these circumstances."

"You're taking what we've all worked our entire careers for, fucking people over, and then repackaging it all for a quick buck at our expense?" she said, her voice rising. Someone at the back of the table stood up. This was Carson's cue to leave. He stood too, and buttoned his coat.

"I thank you all for your time and your exceptional contribution as a member of the MacArthur-Brown family. I wish you nothing but the best of luck, and Tim can answer any of your questions," Carson said, moving backward and out of the board room before the words had even finished leaving his mouth.

* * * * * * *

On the way out of the building, the burner phone rang again. First, Carson spoke into his wrist.

"Car," he said. Then he snapped open the phone and held to his
ace; his voice dropped to a harsh whisper. "I told you, I'm on the way.
's done. Just hang on, I can't have anyone here knowing that-"

"Sir?"

Carson looked up. Tim had caught up and was standing behind him
vith his arms spread wide, questioning. "I'll call you back," Carson said.

"Sir, can I ask what just happened? You blindsided me with a
everance package for the VPs, claiming cost-cutting that we don't need,
nd now you're out here talking – who were you talking to? Is
omething happening that I should know about?" Tim asked.

Tim's face had gone so crimson he looked as if he might have a
eart attack. The cold easterly wind was whipping their overcoats
round like flags lowered to half-mast. Though they were out in the open
ir again, the wind in his face, the ceiling of thick gray clouds overhead,
nd the incessant protests from his assistant made Carson feel as if he
ould not breathe. Everyone he came in contact with, and everything he
nteracted with, somehow, was making him feel at fault, as if each
roblem in the world - no matter how miniscule or unsolvable - was his
luty to address and of his making.

"Sir," Tim said again, forcefully. Scolding. "If something improper or illegal is happening…" Tim began.

"Fucking *shut* it, Tim," he shouted. He could not help himself; the pressure had been building for who knew how long. Before he knew what was happening, Carson could feel his next words escape him. "I don't want to hear it right now, or again. I want you to go back to the office and pack your things."

He'd expected Tim's mouth to hang open, for shock to drain the blood from his body like a vampire. Instead his features tightened, and his fists clenched at his sides and then released. Suddenly, Carson wished for the car very much. NODs were nearly instantaneous much of the time. He could barely imagine the odds of this - the one time he was about to get strangled on a busy sidewalk in broad daylight - being the one time in history the car got stuck in a period of particularly high travel volume.

Just as he thought to take a step back, his wrist chimed helpfully and the red, low-slung sedan glided soundlessly to park an inch from the curb. The car hissed for an instant as the cabin depressurized, and a previously unremarkable section of the smooth side of the vehicle slid to the side to reveal an interior of leather couches and touch screens emerging pleasantly from power-saving mode. Carson glanced behind him and dropped his briefcase on the couch just inside the vehicle, and turned back to Tim. Tim's face was not devastated - no, he was motivated. Carson felt compelled to depart as quickly as possible.

"Judy will assist you with anything you need," Carson said. He tried to bring his tone down to be consoling and understanding. He was realizing the potential error of what he had just lashed out and done. "It's just not a good match right now, Tim. We're going to have more situations like this when news of the cure goes wide, and we just can't have any uncertainty if we're going to getting ready to go before the-"

Tim turned and walked down the street without another word before Carson could finish. His stride was purposeful, as if he knew precisely where he was going next. Carson watched him for a moment and then climbed in the car, relaxing against the ergonomically designed backrest. He sighed.

"Well," he said. "I guess that makes what - fifteen people who want me dead? I've lost count."

There was a small green cursor blinking on the touch screen across the car from where he sat, waiting patiently for instruction. The car was perfectly air-conditioned and comfortable. He felt safe and relaxed again; it was a sense of relief he'd built over years of relying upon the latest model of the NO-Driver autonomous vehicle in any weather, hour or situation. Employees, business deals, even family members – they could each turn on you with no warning. NODs took you where you told them to every single time. They followed orders unquestioningly.

"Let's go to the airport," he said. "One more trip to make and then I think it'll be time for a nice, long vacation."

*"**Beginning trip to: the Airport,**"* the car's pleasant, feminine voice intoned. The vehicle rocketed away from the curb at sixty miles an hour, but Carson barely felt the movement at all. He had just one more stop to make before everything would be settled.

* * * * * * *

In ten minutes they had left the narrow thoroughfares of downtown Manhattan, smoothly accelerating up a widely curving on ramp that joined a two lane highway. Carson's vehicle veered left, joining a caravan of other identically designed cars traveling within inches of each other, hurtling down the road as part of one long train. Every few seconds the caravan would pass an exit and several dozen cars, in perfect, effortless synchronization, would break off from the larger group, assume a smaller-packed formation ,and dart off the highway into the city's heart again.

To watch the action from a distance, from an approaching airliner r from the top floor of an overlooking building, was to observe an awe-1spiring dance of cooperative movement, in which each moment 2emed destined to bring a disastrous collision from a car swerving too lose to another or stopping short suddenly and causing a pile-up of ozens - perhaps hundreds - of others. Yet the hub of interconnected avigational computers, communicating with each other instantaneously bout speed, direction, incoming obstacles, road conditions, and any ther possible data point made certain that accidents never - not rarely, ot every once in a while, but *never* - occurred. After the introduction of JODs twenty years earlier - which, to Carson, felt like generations onger - the only thing that could cause a traffic accident of any kind was n impossible incidence of bad luck such as a bridge collapsing, the 1ovement of the tectonic plates, a hidden volcano exploding from eneath the surface of the Earth.

So Carson did not pay attention when he rode anywhere anymore; he car became a place where he could get work done, calling to check n the status of initiatives, instructing managers as to the course of ction with a test procedure, inquiring with friends on various ongressional committees, or making any other sort of communication e needed to in order to ensure his professional life proceeded as moothly as ever. The red NOD was his mobile office, and he savored his highly efficient, highly private luxury. And, he savored the ability to use his vehicle to conduct business somewhat outside the bounds of what was good and proper.

He felt the burner phone in his pocket. He'd been ignoring it, because even touching the phone in the wrong moments triggered an annoying psychological reaction; he felt unnecessary guilt, unreasonable suspicion, even a warmth to the touch that he swore got worse as he fixated on it, like someone had left a warm tap running for too long.

He exhaled deeply and stared outside, looking in the windows of the cars in the other lane. Directly across from his own vehicle was one in which Carson could see the silhouette of two people sitting side by side, and as he watched a woman nestled her head on the shoulder of the man. He cleared his throat reflexively, as if something had suddenly caught there. Feeling watched again, he spoke to the nav computer.

"Distance to destination," he said.

The green cursor blinked thoughtfully for three beats, and then the even voice: *"Five,"* it said.

It took a second for this to compute in Carson's mind. He mouth opened a little, forming a tiny confused circle. It was certainly possible ne nav had misheard his request; brief miscommunications in speech ecognition happened every now and again. He spoke again.

"Computer. Distance to destination, *please*." As if being polite would help alleviate whatever temporary misfiring circuitry had caused ne problem.

"*Five, four*," the computer read.

"Computer," Carson began, unsure of what else to say. He could ot remember the recalibration protocol commands. He'd never in two ecades needed them.

"*Three, two*," it continued in the same patient monotone.

Carson held his breath, trapped in his own stunned dismay. A ountdown?

"*One*."

* * * * * * *

The green cursor disappeared and the touchscreens at the front of he vehicle went bright white, like exploding flash bulbs, before the white collapsed upon itself. Carson shielded his eyes. The green cursor was restored for a last moment, and then it expanded to fill the entire screen, three feet high and five feet wide, in front of where Carson sat. He had scrambled backward to occupy the leather couch furthest away from the screen, and now he stared in confusion at the display. He was struck by childhood memories of computers flashing error screens, erupting into blue backgrounds and white lines of indecipherable code just before powering down. He'd never seen such things in his adult life but the memories were still there, and they came to him now vividly. The cursor stopped blinking. The black space at its center faded, like blinds being opened, and Carson found himself staring into the gaunt, liver-spotted face of a stranger.

"Good afternoon, Mr. Phillips," the stranger said, in a croaking, nicotine-soaked voice. He wore wire-framed, thin glasses that sat halfway down his nose; the impression was of a librarian or a tax collector. At the very least, Carson could not help feel, that even after four words, he was being condescended to - that this person thought very little of him before he'd even said anything.

He could not think of much that was worthwhile to say, though, and so he mumbled, marveling: "What the hell is this?"

"This is an important opportunity," the stranger said. He leaned forward as if he were taking part in a job interview or an interrogation. This is a chance for you to quickly, painlessly secure your safety by answering a series of very basic, very clear questions."

Confusion evolved into disbelief. This old ghoul was trying to *threaten* him. In a millisecond, Carson's shock and fear were gone, replaced by indignation. "You're fucking threatening me? You have no idea who you're dealing with, pal. Tell me your goddamn name, because you going to have a *world* of shit come down on your head for this," he said. He could feel the heat in his cheeks now, and for once, that felt good.

The stranger looked down, at something out of the frame, and shook his head slowly. Ruefully. Bemused.

"My name is Alexei, Mr. Phillips, and I assure you, I know quite enough. I know, for instance, precisely who you are, and I'm very much aware of MacArthur-Brown, and the merger. I know what you have at stake to lose, and I know that you need my help."

"That's fantastic. Best of luck to you," Carson said. He tired quickly of people wasting his time. "Nav computer, place call to city police."

He waited, watching for the reappearance of the blinking cursor and the comforting, familiar chime. It did not come; instead, he heard the disappointed sigh from the bald stranger on the screen. There was a chime then, but it sounded garbled and broken, as if transmitted through a busted speaker. A panel on the front console slid to the side and a steering wheel slid outward; Carson could not disguise his shock at seeing such an antiquated piece of equipment as a means for manually piloting a car. Perhaps Alexei read his features then.

"I see now, regrettably, that I must demonstrate to you the depth of my commitment," Alexei said. There was a practiced quality to the words that made Carson's stomach clench suddenly with anxiety; it was as if Alexei had gained extreme comfort with these words simply through repeating them dozens - perhaps thousands - of times. "This is simply to expedite the process, Mr. Phillips, I assure you."

He briefly caught sight of the steering wheel jerking violently of its own accord.

The car swerved to the left, the front end colliding with another car with a terrific scream of metal scraping against metal. Carson tumbled backward, his legs flying up in front of his face, and he rolled up against the side of the door handle, smashing his head on plastic. His vision flashed briefly gray and he gasped for air, his hands flailing out at his

des for purchase. A cacophony of warning chimes erupted outside
Carson's car, and the other automated vehicles slammed on their breaks
behind him to provide extra space or accelerated forward to distance
themselves from Carson's inexplicably erratic movements. In the next
second the car jerked back the other way, into its lane again, and
returned to normal speed and behavior just as Carson was sent
somersaulting forward, mashing his face into the seat and then landing
on all fours on the floor of the interior.

He remained there, moaning, for another moment, trying to stop
the world from spinning around him and already feeling throbbing in his
neck and the back of his skull. He could hear Alexei chuckling. Carson
felt furious, frightened, and alone; he could only assume that Alexei was
totally in control of the car, in control of the navigational computer.
Which leaves me with what, exactly? He thought.

"It doesn't give me pleasure, these situations," Alexei said. "Not
much, that is."

"Fuck off," Carson muttered, spitting on the floor. His mouth
tasted like blood.

"However, I will say that it thrills me - it fills me with an awe-
inspiring sense of *purpose* - to help people in situations like yourself. To

assist those who need their slates washed clean, who need to be forgiven for their sins," Alexei said.

"I don't have the slightest idea what you're talking about," Carson said.

Carson looked up from the floor and caught Alexei smiling down benevolently from the touch screen.

"Do you know the first step in being forgiven for your sins, Mr. Phillips? It's *confession*." He could not have looked more pleased. While Carson's life had suddenly spiraled out of control, from Alexei's perspective everything was falling neatly into place, as it doubtlessly had many times before, just as planned, like effortlessly coordinated fast-moving traffic. "Now, Carson. Let's confess."

* * * * * * * *

"Confess what?" Carson asked. He was half worried about what, exactly, he was expected to admit, but other items had clouded his mind. As a company president, it had long paid off for him to be relentlessly pragmatic and forward-thinking, and in this very moment that instinct served him well. It pointed him to one imperative: finding a way out.

There was the burner phone in his pocket, but it seemed impossible that Alexei would allow him to make a call to the police without some sort of immediate retribution. He had to find another way.

The NOD was potentially the instrument of his own demise now, but even self-driving cars had been designed with safety features. The efficiency and effectiveness of the vehicles over the decades had made these safety measures taken for granted and mostly out of the masses' consideration, but Carson knew they existed. There were ways to stop a car that had malfunctioned; though, Carson reasoned, the people he was dealing with had likely thought of that and may have taken control of that mechanism, too. If they could control the steering, the communications, and the acceleration and braking, that meant they controlled just about everything digital there was. *That* meant that his hope lay with anything not connected to the network.

Like the manual door release, his mind offered, helpfully. It did not, however, provide him with an option as to what exactly he was supposed to do once he escaped from a vehicle that was traveling down a crowded interstate at over a hundred miles an hour.

Alexei spoke.

"You must admit the truth about the wrong you have done," he said. "I am above all things a man of my word, Mr. Phillips, and I make you this solemn promise: the moment you admit your sin, this will all be over."

With his oily appearance and unpleasant smirk, Carson's new friend Alexei did not seem the type to simply let bygones be bygones once he'd started to spill his guts on – *well, there's another question*, he thought. *What does he want me to admit to?* He had to get to the manual release; it was, if Carson remembered correctly, beneath the front steering wheel. He had to stall, and then, eventually, he had to make his move. For now he stalled.

"I…I know I have to admit what I've done," he said. "I feel awful about everything, and I owe you my sincere apology," Carson said, staring meaningfully into Alexei's thin face. He appeared frozen for a millisecond.

"Wrong," Alexei said.

An invisible, digital foot stomped on the vehicle's brakes, and this time Carson pitched forward without warning, his face colliding with the plastic of the front console. Tears sprang to his eyes and he felt like his face was on fire; he knew instantly, through the terrific pain, that his

ose had been shattered. He gasped for breath as the car accelerated
gain, slamming on his back against the seat and listening to the alarm
ells all around him. When he opened his eyes, dazedly, Alexei was
laring.

"Do not do that. I assure you that we are not engaged in a game,
Mr. Phillips," he said. "You have two more chances."

Carson glanced out the side of the car and he could see that the
ther vehicles now were keeping their distance permanently, having
udged through some indecipherable algorithm that his car was a risk too
reat to approach. He was alone on the road, and alone inside the
ehicle. His mind raced through choices he'd made, mistakes that had
iled up; they were a seemingly natural reaction to the pain, the awful,
nfair pain emanating throughout his head and downward in waves
cross his body.

He tried to imagine who could be out to strike at him. The list, he
ealized miserably, was long. He thought of Tim, stalking down the
treet, nursing a recent wound and whatever grudges he may have
ecretly harbored. He pictured employees from Brenner Labs anguished
nd wishing for his death. He considered his competitors, those who
vould be left in the dust after the announcement of the Brenner Labs and

MacArthur Brown merger and the resulting cancer gene therapy that would be brought to market.

It had to be a competitor; there were few he could fathom with the resources to assault the digital defenses of the navigational computer system and assert this kind of control. To do so required money, staff, time, care, and a personal investment, no doubt, in seeing him brought low.

"Mr. Phillips?" Alexei asked, politely. "We haven't much time. A second try?"

Fuck it, Carson thought. If it meant his life, they could have the tools with which to arm themselves and draw blood from his employer. It was only a job, after all. He had his family to consider – his future. "Fine," Carson said, the words coming out slurred and stuffy with running blood. "I admit it. To push through the merger, we bribed Feds. People at the Justice Department. I can name names. Just tell me where to do it and I will," Carson said. "Now please let me go."

The steering wheel jerked violently right, and Carson flew into the side of the door. He heard a sickening crack from his side, and fresh agony lit up his side from his wrist to his shoulder. A broken arm, erhaps bruised ribs. They did not want the information about the ayoffs.

"Alexei," he begged. "Tell me what you want, and I can say it or et it for you. I don't know what you're looking for, but I can help. I'm a owerful man. Please."

The car engaged in several more sequences of rapid turns left and ien right, right and then left; each time Carson tumbled across the iterior, his injuries increasingly severe, his body protesting weakly. A ow, pathetic cooing noise escaped from his lips, and he began to cry.

"I admit it, all of it," he said. "The bribes. We cheated on corporate ixed and paid off lobbyists. We bought elections. I skimmed money off ie top of severance packages for a thousand different firings. We onducted testing of our own version of the cure on kids – it killed ome."

He wasn't even crying at physical pain, now. He was lying in the ack of the car, bleeding and broken, and wishing for mercy. Wishing or one more chance to return to his family; he imagined Claire's face. Kelly cross-legged in bed, examining him as he worked at his desk.

"I'm begging you, Alexei," he said.

Alexei seemed to consider what he'd said, and for a brief moment, Carson could imagine that perhaps he'd squeezed enough out of him. He'd endured all that he would be forced to. He had taken enough.

Then Alexei shook his head sadly.

"Mr. Phillips, I have stopped counting chances, but I haven't stopped counting miles," he said. "We have reached, if you'll look out the window, the bridge overlooking the bay. It is several hundred feet down to the surface of the water. You see how the afternoon sun, cutting through the clouds, reflects in that way? It is quite beautiful, you must admit."

Distantly, Carson nodded.

"Yes, I agree as well. I am glad I could share this moment with you, because I have agreed, in contrast with my usual methods of practice, to allow my employer to speak with you directly. I am disappointed I could not hear your confession directly, but I trust this experience will, in the end, have served its purpose."

He straightened his tie, nodded, and was gone from the camera. The back of a black chair was revealed, where Alexei had been sitting. For a moment there was nothing – nothing save the sound of the car's efficient, electric hum as it proceeded across the bridge. He looked out the window, unable to move, his eyelids fluttering. He glanced at the guardrail that separated the edge of the road from open air.

Strangely, the NOD's on-board voice returned then, and it began speaking to him soothingly. It began to address him by name, as if they had known each for many years. He supposed that in a way they had, but still, it was an odd thing to-

No.

"Baby," Kelly said from the screen in front of him. "Oh, honey."

He looked at her, dimly.

"I tried to give you a chance to tell the truth. So many chances, in fact," she said.

"What are you – Kelly? What's happening?"

She looked at him with the most peculiar expression; there was an almost parental love cast across her face, which seemed youthful and refreshed, relieved of a great burden. Kelly seemed to be seeing him from a thousand miles above, looking down from a cloud.

"We told you from the beginning that we wanted you to admit your sin," she said. "Nothing more than that. And even to the end, you couldn't."

"But I told you everything," he said, pleading. Unable to comprehend.

She smiled at him warmly. "The phone in your pocket," Kelly said.

Oh my God. Mary mother of Christ.

"Tell me this – and do it quickly, because in a moment I have to go and join our daughter on the couch. We're going to be watching some cartoons that she's been waiting patiently for. But tell me now: do you want to call her once more before the end? Do you want to hear her voice a last time? Or is it possible that mine – just once – the voice of your *wife* is enough?"

He felt the car accelerating smoothly, away from the fast-approaching sirens behind him. The windows went down at once, so that air screamed throughout the vehicle like it was in the heart of a great, clear tornado. It veered right, toward the guard rail.

Carson did imagine Brie's face once then, in passing, amongst a thousand others that he had briefly intersected with and then discarded after they had served their use or grown inconvenient. It was tragic, in a way that she did not elicit more in him, or that no one did. It was certainly more tragic than the approach of the guard rail, the open air, the descent. His baptism.

He thought of one last thing – to call out to Claire and even to Kelly, to apologize to them with a few words that they would recall later and perhaps take some solace from. There had to be something he could say that would repair the damage he now, for the first time, realized that he had done. In the last instant, he thought to tell them both that he loved them, to shout out the words as loud as he could against the roar of the wind and the sound of the collision.

But Kelly had already hung up.

31986946R00081

Made in the USA
Middletown, DE
18 May 2016